THE SAHARAN QUEEN

A PREQUEL NOVELLA TO THE VISIGOTHS OF SPAIN SERIES

PAULA CONSTANT

FEHU PRESS

For Chloe

SAHARAN AFRICA AD 670

MAP OF NORTH AFRICA AND SOUTHERN SPAIN WITH RELEVANT PLACE NAMES

1

THE SAHARAN QUEEN

Saharan Africa, AD 670
Near Kairouan, modern day Tunisia

Her name is legend: Al Kahinat. The Arab scholars like to write of their victories, and defeating her was one of their greatest. But they do not write of the woman, Dahiya, nor the girl she once was. Already the truth fades, the lie of her legend arising to take its place in their books and songs. Men always call lie that which they do not understand; Dahiya told me that herself, once, long ago, when we were Riders together and the Arabs fled before our swords. You are children, and the summer days are long. Sit by me and listen well, for the tale I tell is your own.

It is the tale of every girl who dares to dream.
The Lady of Aurariola, to her granddaughters
Al Andalus, AD 752

They came upon the Arab camp at dusk, when the desert wind had ceased and the sky turned to flame.

"A hundred men, maybe more," murmured Tabat. He

lay on his belly in a shallow depression barely a hundred paces from the camp.

"What are they doing?" Lying next to her father, Dahiya watched the men from beneath the indigo cloth of her *tagelmust*, which she wore wound about her face and head as the men did.

"Praying," he said briefly. Tabat was a man of few words. Here in Tripolitana they were far from their own lands, and his words were even fewer as a result. They had come because men spoke of a great army that had landed to the east and moved like a plague across the desert. Tabat had led his Riders to find this army, for the Jerawa had never waited for an enemy to come to them.

Dahiya watched the Arabs kneel and place their heads to the ground. She thought it was a strange way to pray. Her people, the Jerawa, worshipped at places where their gods lived still: places of water, which all desert nomads knew were sacred, or in the tombs and caves of their ancestors.

Tabat took another sharp look at the praying men, inching backward until he was certain they were out of sight. He, Dahiya, and the rest of the scouting party slipped into the gloaming and silently made their way back to where their camels and the rest of the men waited.

Tabat squatted on his haunches, Dahiya at his side, and the men followed suit. They did not light a fire. The Jerawa rode hard, in the deep sands where wood was scarce and food hard to find. They sometimes boasted that a man of their ranks could live three days on one date alone: a day to suck the skin, another to feast on the flesh, and one more to drain the last taste from the stone.

"We will take them in the early hours," said Tabat. He looked at the watchful circle of faces. "They have six to every man of ours. We must wait until they sleep and move swiftly."

One of his Riders spoke up. "This is the army we search for, then?"

"A part of it, perhaps." Tabat looked sceptical. "But not the whole. I will capture a man and make him speak of where the rest lies."

He outlined what each must do. The men listened respectfully, then went to rest amongst their couched and hobbled camels.

"You have your bow, Dahiya?" Tabat asked when they had gone.

She nodded and held up the weapon, the recurved ends of which she had hewn from bone when she was a child smaller than the bow itself.

"You will aim your arrows from the place we lay today," he said. "When you see the first flames rise from the camp, begin. Take as many as you can. But as soon as men come toward you, retreat back to the camels, Dahiya, and ride to the place we designated. Do you understand?"

Dahiya nodded. Her father was restless, already half engaged in the battle to come, and her only job now was to obey.

She lay wrapped in camel blankets, staring up at the crystalline night, knowing she would not sleep. Around her the men of the Jerawa lay still, though she knew they, too, did not sleep.

In the small hours, they rose and moved silently through the night. Tabat nodded at his daughter, then he and the men were gone, and Dahiya was alone behind the dune.

She drew her bow and pulled a long arrow from the quiver, working it back and forth between her fingers and the string in an unconscious gesture as she watched the sleeping Arabs.

Waiting.

She felt the moment when blood first fell, though no sound cut the air. It was a feeling, a ripple in the night, that only those born to the desert silence might know. She saw the faint movement of a shadow, and another.

Then a garbled cry hurt the night, and the first flames rose from the other side of the camp.

It was time.

Dahiya drew her breath with the arrow. Then she released it, and a man fell.

Another took his place. The Arabs wore heavy, embroidered robes easily seen in the night. The Jerawa's thin indigo cloth was dark and indiscernible, Tabat and his men no more than strange shadows rising from the ground. Dahiya drew and breathed in the steady rhythm that had long been part of her soul, letting the arrows flow through her fingers like water over rock.

As flames licked higher on the wooden crates stacked under hessian covering, Dahiya saw fear etched on the Arabic faces as they swung wildly at the deadly shadows. But Tabat had trained his men well, and they disappeared as suddenly as they had come, taking a man with a knife here, another with an arrow there. Amidst it all, Dahiya's arrows rained down in a steady stream, taking a man with every shot.

She heard a hoarse cry and turned to see an Arab pointing in her direction. She did not wait to send another arrow but slid back, as her father had ordered, running low and silently to where the camels remained couched. She untied the leg rope of the first with deft movements and mounted it. The camel lurched to its feet and the others, tied nose to tail, followed. They were packed and alert, waiting only for the signal.

Dahiya urged the train forward and they slipped between the dunes, walking in the slow, unhurried pace that could continue all night. She had no fear of being followed. Her father's men would leave none alive to come after her. And besides, she had heard that the Arabs did not venture alone into the sands. They feared what lived there, as well they should. The Arabs did not belong on the soil of Africa.

They never would.

Dahiya finally saw the clump of acacia trees she was looking for, and she couched the camels.

She did not have long to wait.

The men slipped into the trees like wisps of dark cloud blown in on the desert night. Some limped, others clutched their sides, but when the camels rose and moved silently into the dunes, untied now and each carrying a Rider, only two saddles were empty.

Tabat rode at the head of their band, and he led them a way Dahiya did not know. Despite the darkness and the tagelmust covering his face, she sensed her father's tension. The mood after an attack was often sombre – but tonight, there was something different. She had never known Tabat ride so far and hard when only death lay behind them.

As the first pale glimmer of dawn washed the sky, they couched the camels once more.

"We go on foot," Tabat murmured. "And carefully. We none of us must be seen."

They followed his silent passage up a steep cliff, covered in coarse desert grasses and hard rocky edges, a path none would willingly take. They climbed high, and Dahiya was panting as the path widened to a hard plateau. She dropped to her belly as the men had and inched her way to the edge.

Then she drew her breath, understanding her father's tension.

Far below, spread across the plain, was a camp greater than anything she had ever seen. Line upon line of sleeping men littered the ground, so many Dahiya could not count them. Camels grazed far into the distance, and she felt angry at the loss of the precious grasses upon which her people depended.

"It is a horde," whispered one of the men wonderingly. "Like a sea. None could defeat such an army."

"How many?" whispered another. "How many are there?"

Tabat's face was grim. "The man I killed," he said quietly, "told me there are more than ten thousand."

There was a collective gasp.

"They are led by a man named Uqba ibn Nafi," Tabat went on. He stared down at the plain below, and Dahiya shivered at the cold fury in her father's eyes.

"If we do not find a way to defeat this army," said Tabat, "the Jerawa – and all the Amazigh people – will be destroyed and our land lost forever."

The pale desert sun painted the day into being, and Dahiya lay amongst the men of her blood, watching the Arabic enemy who dared dream of taking her country.

2

LOVE'S DARKNESS

**AD 672 – Two Years Later
Saharan Africa
Kingdom of Aures - Modern day Algeria**

You ask if I believe in love at first sight, but you speak of romance, not love. You know nothing of love's dark power. Your fine young men and their pretty smiles are a game to be played on summer fields, beneath sunlit skies. You live a life that asks no more of you than such games. But all women must learn love's darkness eventually, though they may think it a summer field at the start.

*The Lady of Aurariola, to her granddaughters
Al Andalus, AD 752*

Her father's sword was named Ahar, and it had never been wielded by a woman.

"Women can rule," said Dahiya, eyeing the blade longingly. "Tin Hinan was queen of her *kel*. Men still tell stories of her."

"They were different days." Tabat, Dahiya's father and *amgar* of

6

Kel Jerawa, sharpened Ahar with long, steady strokes. The name Ahar meant "Lion" in the Amazigh language.

"I wonder what Tin Hinan's sword was called," said Dahiya, watching him work.

"Even Tin Hinan could not have wielded a blade such as Ahar."

Her father held the sword upright and examined the edge. It gleamed in the hard Saharan sunlight. "No woman is strong enough to use a war sword in battle. Tin Hinan would have had men to fight for her, even if they called her queen. Women are not meant to lead men into battle. They are meant to welcome them when they return."

Tabat was a tall man, broad at the shoulder, with the deep-set dark eyes and high cheekbones typical of the Amazigh. The indigo folds of his tagelmust were looped about his neck. Beneath them was a jewelled amulet containing relics from his forefathers. They, too, had led the Jerawa, and their strength ran through his veins.

He placed the sword to one side and touched Dahiya's face.

"This *siyala*," he said, tracing the pattern that ran from her bottom lip to her chin, "is of far greater importance than wielding a sword ever could be. Its seeds resemble the sons you will bear the Jerawa. Sons to fight the Arabs who come to our shores, driving them from Africa forever, so we may restore the kingdom of Altava to its rightful place and rule ourselves, as is our destiny.

"We are Imazighen," he said, smiling at his daughter. "Our very name means 'free men'. Your sons will live to see their kingdom born again, and you will be the mother of all, just as Tin Hinan once was."

Dahiya was not appeased.

"You do not know that Tin Hinan didn't fight," she said stubbornly.

Tabat's smile faded. "Enough, Dahiya."

When her father used her full name, she knew she had pushed him as far as he would go.

"You are no longer a child," he said curtly, nodding at the siyala on her chin. "Soon men will dance for your favour, and you will take a husband. You are my only child. The man who marries you will be proud to have such a woman bear his sons. It is time you ceased dreaming of carrying the Lion into battle, Dahiya, and turned your thoughts instead to the cubs you will carry in your arms."

Seeing her mutinous expression, his face softened. "You will still be a queen, Daya," he said. "We honour our wives as no other men do. Tin Hinan did not need to carry iron against her enemies. The wisdom she possessed carried her tribe out of the wastelands when her enemies thought them dead and buried in the sands. The sons she bore wreaked revenge on those enemies and built a new kingdom. You will choose your husband carefully and use your wisdom to ensure his victories. Then your sons will lead the Jerawa, and perhaps other kels also. You know my dream, Daya. You are still the one I rely upon to see it made manifest."

"Altava," she breathed, her amber eyes glowing in the afternoon light. "We will form an *amenokal*, a confederation of the Amazigh, and together we will build a kingdom mightier even than Tin Hinan's."

"And you will be its queen." Tabat pinched her chin, smiling at her indulgently. "But first" – he wagged a finger at her – "we must find you a husband. And I may have a candidate to interest you."

Dahiya frowned. "Not Igider. He has been following me ever since you returned from the battle at Kairouan, limping whenever I am close so I can be sure not to miss the wound in his leg. Which," she added, "is barely a wound at all, but only a scratch."

"Ah." Tabat grinned. "Do not fault a man for showing you he does not run from a fight. Igider is young, and boastful, but he is also a good warrior. Men follow him. You could do worse than consider him." He held up a defensive hand at her indignation. "But no, my Daya, it is not Igider to whom I refer."

He shot his daughter a sideways look. "The man I wish you to meet is called Ilyan," he said. "He has Amazigh blood, speaks our language, and understands our ways."

Dahiya frowned. "A foreigner?"

"Not quite. Ilyan speaks the language of the Goths across the sea in Spania, and he has worn the emperor's uniform, that of the Greek fleet, the *Karabisianoi*. But he has Amazigh blood, of that there can be no doubt. He also has allies in many places, and he speaks more tongues than I knew existed."

"Then he is a foreigner," said Dahiya, with palpable disdain.

"No." Tabat shook his head decisively. "Whatever his lineage – and none, I suspect, will ever truly know it – Ilyan is of Africa. He knows the peoples of our land, and their conflicts, better than any man alive. He is barely more than twenty years, and yet already he claims the title of count and is governor of Septem, the western-most port on our coast and perhaps the most important. And" – he gave his daughter a knowing smile – "it is rumoured that he seeks a wife from amongst the Amazigh."

"You wish for me to meet this Ilyan."

Dahiya spoke in a flat tone. Although she was barely sixteen, Dahiya was almost of a height with Tabat, and whilst she was not quite so broad as her father, none would call her small. She was lithe and strong and moved with the same fluid grace her father did. When she drew her bowstring her arrows inevitably found their mark, and it would be a brave man who would come upon her unaware in her tent after dark, as she could wield the narrow blade at her waist with lethal dexterity.

"I do." Tabat reached over and pushed the thin material *tasuwart* from her head, exposing the heavy coil of midnight hair. He pulled it free from the carved wooden pin that held it and let the black waves cascade down through his fingers.

"Ilyan rides to Carthage," he said, "to meet with the ships of the Greek fleet, said to be arriving when the lion's moon dies and that of the virgin takes its place. I will ride to meet them. If we are to thrust the Arab invaders from our soil once and for all, we shall need their alliances. You will ride with me."

Dahiya could not suppress a tremor of excitement. She loved the dramatic cliffs of the Awras Mountains, the ochre glow of the desert sun upon stone, and the steep ravines in which their goats and camels grazed. But Carthage was the greatest port on their coast, a city of legendary treasures. She could imagine nothing more exciting than to visit it – except, perhaps, the prospect of adding her voice to those who advised her father at council. To be a part of her father's vision – of the conversations in which nations were built and fates decided – *this*, thought Dahiya exultantly, *is what matters. Not which men will dance for my favour. Not who I will take to my bed.*

Such things could never be more important, to me, than Altava, than building my father's dream.

"We will leave two days from now." Tabat sheathed Ahar in its plain silver scabbard, closed the leather flap over it with a jewelled nail, and wrapped his tagelmust with deft movements. "You will prepare what we need for the journey. We will not ride alone."

He gave his daughter a half smile.

"Igider will accompany us," he said, unable to hide his amusement at Dahiya's contemptuous expression. "Zdan, too, for he is a warrior equal to Igider. Both are possible leaders of the Jerawa after I am gone. You will treat them with the respect they deserve."

Dahiya shrugged. "I like Zdan. He thinks before he speaks."

Seeing the expression on her father's face, she said warningly, "I did not say I wished to marry him, Baba, just that I liked him."

Her father shrugged. "Many marriages are made on less."

"I thought you wanted me to marry this Ilyan?"

"I want you to meet him." Her father had begun to walk away. "Besides," he called back over his shoulder, laughing, "I am not at all certain that Ilyan will wish to marry *you*."

* * *

It is not that I do not wish to marry, Dahiya thought as they rode out two days later, *but rather that I want more than just marriage.*

The dawn was no more than a steel thread on the horizon. They rode camels through sands silent with night damp, stars high and bright above. The predawn smelled heady and wild. It was the scent of the desert – and freedom. Dahiya had spent nights beneath the mud roofs of the mountain villages where the women, children, and old men of their kel rested. But she was her father's daughter, raised in the sands amongst the warriors he led, and did not enjoy the restrictions of the walled oases known to the Amazigh as *adwwar*.

It might have been different, had her mother lived.

But Safiyya had died in a night of blood and horror when Dahiya was barely four years old. Young as she had been, even now Dahiya could close her eyes and smell the smoke of her adwwar burning, hear her mother whisper: *Run, Lalla; run, and do not stop.*

Run Dahiya had, but not before she had seen her mother's small knife knocked brutally to the ground, as her killer pushed his way inside, and heard Safiyya's scream of terror fade to silence.

Many of the Jerawa's women and children had died that night. Dahiya hid in the mountains around the adwwar for days until the attackers left. Only when she was sure it was her father's figure she saw leading men into the wreckage of her home did she venture down and stand, trembling and ashamed, before Tabat's broken face.

"I could not save her," she said, her eyes dropping from the pain she saw in his. "I could not —"

Her father's hand over her mouth stilled her words.

"The next time," he said grimly, "you will be ready. A warrior never regrets his defeats, Dahiya. He learns from them. You are the daughter of an amgar, and one day your sons will rule our people. I will teach you everything I know, for if I die, still you must live." He gripped her shoulders, staring past her at the sightless eyes and decaying flesh of his wife. "This was not your fault," he said. "But when we find the men who did this, yours will be the revenge, my Dahiya, for vengeance belongs to the wronged — and it was your eyes that saw your blood die."

Eight years passed before they found the men who killed her mother. Word had spread that Tabat sought them, and the men had fled far, returning only when they thought enough time had elapsed for their horrors to be forgotten. Much could be taught in eight years, and Tabat had not wasted a day, training his daughter harder and with greater discipline than any of the men he led. At night, when he spoke of strategy, it was Dahiya who sat at his side and listened. When he showed her the secrets of bow and arrow, he tied cloth over her eyes and insisted she shoot blind.

"No woman can wield a man's sword," he taught her, "so you must make the knife your arm and learn to feel it like your own hand."

In eight years, Tabat trained his Riders until he had given the Jerawa the reputation of the most feared kel of all their people, and when the day came for them to face those who had taken their adwwar, the Riders showed no mercy.

When his enemies were on their knees before Tabat, he walked the length of their bowed heads, his daughter at his side.

"Tell me," he said, "which man it was who killed my wife."

Dahiya found the face she would recall for all her days. "This one," she said.

Tabat stared at the man until the other dropped his eyes and began to beg for his life.

Only then did Tabat turn to his daughter. "He is yours," he said simply.

Dahiya had reached for her knife, the slim blade with a handle of resin-blackened cord, a deadly thing she had carried since she was strong enough to hold it. She stared into the man's eyes.

"You killed my mother," she said softly. "Your life is mine."

She had watched the life fade from his eyes, had allowed herself to feel the finality of it, for all knew that true revenge must be wholly known and owned, that it may then be released into the sands and not roam as a ghost to sing men into madness. When it was done, she had washed her blade beneath moving water, then baked it in sand at the sun's zenith until it gleamed new.

Her father had not married again, and though she knew he took women when he wished, none of them had borne him sons. When he died, the Jerawa would choose the new amgar from their own ranks, as they would whether Tabat had sons or not. As his daughter, Dahiya would be honoured – but she would never be amgar, could not ask men to support her claim. The man she married, however, would be well positioned to lead. Dahiya's counsel would continue to be valued, and her sons would be raised to take her father's place as amgar.

She wished it could be enough.

Zdan rode ahead of her, slender and watchful. He was a good man and had been her friend from infancy. But she could not imagine sharing his blankets.

In contrast to Zdan's quiet, lithe figure, Igider was tall and loud, with flashing eyes and a wide smile. He favoured Dahiya with it now, his tagelmust wound at a jaunty angle as he allowed his leg to touch her own when he passed her. Staring straight ahead, Dahiya ignored him. She had more important matters to think on than Igider's childish ploys for her attention.

In the sands, the Jerawa rode camels, for they were hardy animals who could be sustained for months in the cold season by the moisture-filled plants. Closer to the sea, though, it was horses the Jerawa prized. They kept a herd in a village on the other side of the mountains. Dahiya loved horses, and her skill with them was something even her father acknowledged. Mounted on horseback, Dahiya felt equal to any man, her bow as deadly a weapon as the heavy iron they wielded, able to loose her arrows with a speed and accuracy impossible on the rolling gait of a camel.

Now, though, she feared her days of practising with bow and horse would soon be over, as would the freedom she found in the desert. Women with babies did not ride with the warriors of the Jerawa. They remained behind the thorn-bush and mud walls of the adwwar, rolling couscous and tending the date-palm orchards, grazing the goats that were slaughtered when men returned from battle.

Dahiya's breath constricted her chest at the thought.

She had spent her whole life as the daughter of Tabat the amgar, indulged by men who thought it amusing to watch their chief's daughter shoot an arrow or drill against them with short sword. She had thrown a knife with accuracy long before she had learned to dress her hair.

Now I am to forget all of that, she thought resentfully, *and find my pleasure in the fall of my* tasuwart *and the henna decorations on my hands.*

She shuddered at the thought of being cloistered amongst women as they made the painstaking henna patterns on her skin that took the best part of the day, giggling amongst themselves about the men they loved. Dahiya could not imagine giggling about any man. She had grown up at the fire listening to them talk of battle and strategy and, occasionally, when they drank too much and forgot she was there, of the women they took.

Men offered no mystery to Dahiya.

She knew there were good men who loved their wives, just as there were others who would never love anything more than their own ambition. But whether they loved their women or not, all men, Dahiya knew, loved battle just as much, if not more. Women were but one part of a larger life. A significant part, it was true; children of the Jerawa were adored and indulged. When they left the adwwar, though, the minds of men turned away from the world they left and became entirely focused on the business of the kel: upon allies and foes, confederates and competitors, mutual enemies, and the future of the Amazigh themselves – the kind of world they may, together, create.

These were the matters Dahiya had been raised to contemplate, and matters most women never thought of. Since the marking of her face last summer with the siyala proclaiming her fertility, Tabat's treatment of her had changed. When they came now to the adwwar, Dahiya was expected to leave the men to talk and join the company of the women instead. She felt awkward and shy in the women's tent, feigning enjoyment in their conversation, all the while feeling a stranger in a strange land.

Whereas this, she thought with savage delight as they rode up a dune into the growing gold of the dawn, *this is where I belong: mounted and riding into the unknown, amongst men who decide their own fate.*

* * *

Two days later, the Jerawa had made camp near a well, but out of sight of it, as was the custom. Dahiya was collecting water when she heard voices in the distance. A party of men was riding toward her. Though they were mounted on camels, she knew at one glance that not all were Amazigh.

Two men rode at the head of the party. One, though clad in desert robes, wore cloth embroidered with thread that glinted in the desert sun and wound his tagelmust in a manner markedly different to the Amazigh. But it was the other man who stood out as a foreigner, making Dahiya draw her breath.

He was taller than the men of the tribes, with hair so golden it seemed to reflect the sun itself. He rode in a short tunic with his legs bare from the thigh down, showing muscle bronzed by the sun. His arms, too, were bare, and they were corded like iron. When he threw back his head and laughed at something his companion said, the sound echoed around the valley.

Dahiya could not take her eyes from him. She had never seen a man clad as he was, baring so much of his body. The sight was as shocking as it was fascinating. She wanted both to touch him and to flee. Instead she stood frozen at the well, oblivious to the water falling from the leather *guerba* she had just laboured to fill.

"Dahiya!" Igider came to stand beside her, frowning at the newcomers. "You should go back to your father," he said. His frown deepened. "And those men should veil themselves."

It was customary for men of the Amazigh to veil, both as protection against evil spirits and out of respect to the women they encountered. The man in the tunic riding toward them, however, showed no discomfort as he came closer, and even had he wished to, he did not possess a tagelmust with which to wind his face.

Ignoring Igider's warning, Dahiya stepped forward with her hand over her heart as she murmured the traditional greetings: Are you well? Are the people of your kel well? Have you had a good journey? Good grazing on the way? Good water? What have you seen on the way?

"I am Dahiya, daughter of Tabat," she said at the end of the long litany of rapidly repeated questions and responses. "You are welcome in my father's camp."

It was not the foreigner who answered, but the man clad in the embroidered desert robes.

"I am Count Ilyan, governor of Septem." He leaned forward, face sharp with interest as he looked at her. He was almost painfully thin, with piercing eyes that moved restlessly and a wild shock of dark hair that rose from his head, giving him a perpetually startled appearance.

"We followed your tracks," he said. "We have been searching for the Riders of the Jerawa for some time."

Dahiya heard his words but gave him no more than a cursory glance, her eyes moving as if of their own volition back to the foreigner at his side.

"Who are *you*?" she said abruptly.

The golden-haired man stared down at her. He had eyes of the most brilliant blue she had ever seen and a face that seemed to radiate the power of the sun itself, as if someone had lit a fire within him that pulsed outward, heating all it touched.

"I am Apsimar," he said, speaking in Greek. "I command the *dromons* of the Greek fleet that will lie up for the winter in Carthage."

"My father said the fleet had not yet arrived."

The man inclined his head courteously, but a small smile played about his mouth, and Dahiya had the impression that he was amused by her challenge rather than intimidated.

"Your father was correct. I went ahead with a small force to Septem, to see Ilyan. The rest of the dromons will reach Carthage by the end of the month."

"Septem is a long way from here," said Dahiya. "You have ridden far from your dromons."

"My dromons follow me," Apsimar said with the easy command of a man accustomed to being obeyed. "And it seems," he went on, the smile widening as his eyes roamed her face in a way that made her colour despite herself, "that the long ride was worth taking."

"Ilyan!"

Dahiya heard her father's voice just as she realised that Igider was looking between her and the newcomer with growing hostility. She stepped back as Tabat reached them, lowering her eyes and trying to feign a calm she did not feel.

"We were expecting to find you in Carthage," Tabat greeted Ilyan as the men couched their camels and dismounted. He gripped Ilyan's arm in the Greek fashion and then greeted the visitors in the manner of the tribes, placing his hand over his heart as he acknowledged each man in turn.

"Apsimar," he said, smiling welcome to the Greek commander. "I am ashamed you find us in the camp, rather than in our adwwar, where I might offer you proper hospitality."

"I have become fond of the desert nights." Apsimar moved fluidly from his camel to Tabat's side, his eyes never leaving Dahiya's face. She felt a tingling in her spine that left her breathless. It was as if she could feel his pulse inside her own.

"I had not realised," he said, coming closer, "how beautiful they could be."

Tabat's smile faded as he looked between Apsimar and his daughter.

"Dahiya," he said in a tone that brooked no opposition, "you may prepare meat for our guests."

She felt Apsimar's eyes like coals on her back as she walked away.

* * *

"I HAVE MET with Kel Awraba and Kel Ifren," Count Ilyan said later that evening. He sat beside Apsimar in a circle of her father's men, cross-legged beneath the desert night, a large plate of camel meat on the ground before them.

Dahiya sat before a tripod, pushing a leather guerba of goats' milk to and fro, making the drink known as *jeera*. She would flavour it with cinnamon and crushed dates when it had thickened. For now, the making of it was defence against Apsimar's keen blue gaze, which she still felt like a brand on her skin.

"And did you form alliances with the Awraba and Ifren?" Tabat asked. He glanced at Dahiya, who was careful to keep her eyes downcast. It would not serve for her father to see the effect Apsimar had upon her.

Ilyan, whilst not of the Jerawa, was, unmistakably, of Ifriquiya; his manners and tongue were easy with those of the tribes, and he sat amongst them as one of their own. Apsimar, by contrast, was breathtakingly foreign. He stood easily a full head taller than Tabat and was half a shoulder wider. Every inch of him was profoundly different to the dark, slight men of the Amazigh. Tabat, Dahiya knew, could never accept such a man paying his daughter attention.

"I made alliance with the Awraba, yes," said Ilyan. "Aksil is a strong leader. He will be a good ally, as you suggested."

He watched Dahiya as he spoke, but with amusement rather than Apsimar's intensity. She had the feeling that Ilyan knew precisely the effect Apsimar had on her. She sensed from the Count of Septem a certain detachment, as if Ilyan would find interest in all people and situations but lose himself in none of them. She liked him.

"And the Ifren?" Tabat asked.

Ilyan frowned. "No," he said shortly. "I met with their leader, Yedder, several days ago. I did not trust him."

"The Ifren are not to be trusted," Igider interjected curtly, and the men around him murmured their agreement.

"I am inclined to agree with you," said Ilyan, favouring Igider with a lazy smile, which disarmed Igider's brash aggression entirely.

Ilyan seemed, Dahiya thought, perpetually amused by them all.

"And you…" Tabat turned courteous but nonetheless hard eyes to Apsimar. "What do you make of the kels? Do you find men with whom you are prepared to fight?"

Apsimar smiled, a slow curve of his mouth that made Dahiya's skin prickle with awareness.

"I will be proud to fight beside the men of the Amazigh," he said. He had a deep, smooth voice clearly accustomed to command, and men turned to him when he spoke. Dahiya had no trouble picturing him at the head of a great force, as she knew he was customarily found. "They appear fierce fighters," Apsimar went on, "and well able to hold back the Arabic force we face."

"If we are to fight beside you," said Tabat, his tone mildly gentler, "we will need horses and weapons. For too long we have held off the Arab invaders with little more than our own hands."

Count Ilyan nodded. "And you have done so admirably," he said. "We come with coin, Tabat, and the resources you need. It is why you find me riding through the sands. I would know what it is you need and will make plans to supply it. If we are to defeat Uqba's forces, we must work together."

As they fell into a discussion of strategy, Dahiya was aware of Apsimar's eyes resting on her face. She mixed dates and cinnamon into the *jeera*, stirring the mixture in a wooden bowl, then pouring it into small glasses, which she passed around the circle of men.

She raised her eyes in time to see Apsimar sip it. He rubbed his lips together appreciatively, smiling at her.

She coloured and looked away.

Late that night, Dahiya lay in her camel blankets beneath the high desert sky, thinking of Apsimar.

When she woke in the morning, he and Ilyan had left, riding for Carthage and the fleet.

"Come," said her father curtly. "We, too, are bound for the coast, though by a different path. War is coming, and Ilyan wishes to co-ordinate the efforts of the tribes with those of the Greek fleet. He will gather some, and I will take the message to others." He gave Dahiya a hard stare. "You ride with us," he said, "but be warned, Dahiya, I will not see you wed the Greek commander. You are Jerawa. We do not leave our homeland – and nor do we allow foreigners to make whores of our daughters."

3

———————

HERESY

The Arabs learn God from their book, and your father's priests take theirs from another. But the desert Amazigh know the gods I was born to, those that live in water and earth and who whisper secrets to those who would listen. I see you frown at such heresy. You glance around uneasily lest a priest hear my blasphemy. I, however, am an old woman, and I fear neither priest nor Arab, for women know things of this earth no man will ever understand.

The Lady of Aurariola, to her granddaughters
Al Andalus, AD 752

On the night the moon grew to half size, the ever-present wind became a storm. The sands whirled, obscuring the sun. The Jerawa couched the camels in a square and hunkered down in their shelter.

A full day and night passed, and still the storm blew. As the second day grew and still the wind howled, men of Kel Ifren appeared like wraiths. Amidst the constant roar, Tabat sat in counsel with Yedder, their leader, who gestured to the ground behind him. When the next brief lull came, the Jerawa followed Yedder's figure through the swirling sands to a deep ravine bordered on either side by sharp cliffs. A small river snaked between them. The path down to the water was steep and rugged.

"Men rarely camp here," said Zdan, looking about uneasily as they picked their way down to the sandy bank at the base.

"Why not?" Igider jostled his camel alongside them. A long-ignored stand of date palms grew on the banks of the shallow river. "It has good water, and grazing. What frightens you, Zdan?"

He winked at Dahiya, who shook her head, rolling her eyes.

"Is the path too difficult for you?" Igider teased. "Afraid you will tumble from your camel?"

Zdan touched his chin to ward off evil and raised his tagelmust over his nose and mouth to prevent spirits from entering his body. "It is a bad place," he muttered, brown eyes sombre.

Igider made a derisive noise and pushed his camel forward, causing Zdan's own to stumble.

Dahiya did not share his amusement. Her people had a long history in the sands. Many places held memories of the past in the soil, known and felt by those who had knowledge of the events that created them. Sometimes the memories were so strong their presence was felt by all men, and those places were marked and avoided. Others may bring bad dreams in the night or illness to the animals.

But sometimes such places could not be avoided. They had been riding in hard winds for days even before the storm had overcome them, and Dahiya was not the only one grateful to be sheltered from the sands. The screaming wind dropped as they descended into the ravine, and men began to converse. They would make a fire tonight, eat meat and fresh dates.

The wind dropped altogether as dusk fell. Dahiya walked out of camp to a place where the water formed a pond. She left her *tasuwart* hanging on the thorn bush so men would know she was bathing in the water beyond. She was not concerned that she would be disturbed. Even Igider, bold as he was, would never transgress the unspoken laws by which they lived. Bathing was private and sacred. Dahiya had never felt concerned that she might be watched.

She shed her linen pantalons and loose tunic and sighed with pleasure as she sank into water still warm from the day's blazing heat. It was the end of the summer months and an ill time to travel, the heat a thing of fury at the height of the day, but it could not be helped if they wished to reach Carthage whilst the fleet, and Ilyan, remained.

An image of Apsimar's golden, burnished body rose in her mind. Dahiya forced it away with an effort. It had sometimes seemed, in the isolation wrought by the winds, that Apsimar was seared upon her memory like a brand on a camel.

She stood up in the water and used the rough olive paste made by women of their adwwar to scrub her body down, feeling the fresh pleasure of the dirt sloughing away with the old skin. She had mixed desert mint and henna with some of the paste, and this she spread through her hair with a comb made of ivory that her father had once taken in battle. Dusk fell with purple stillness as she bathed. High above, a lone bird of prey circled, wings outstretched as it floated on invisible currents.

She had finished bathing and was pulling on her clothes when a faint sound made her swing around, hand on the knife that hung in the thorn bush. Her eyes examined the rippled stone of the cliffs. Shadows moved across them, the light deceptive in the gloaming, but she could not discern any particular threat. She dressed hurriedly, keeping one eye on the cliff face. It struck her that the air had become unusually still. At the distant turn of the ravine, the sky had a heavy, purple cast, nothing like the pearlescent glow of a customary desert dusk. Dahiya shivered with unease, thinking of Zdan's words as she walked back to the encampment.

"We have meat," Igider greeted her, grinning as he indicated the bird carcasses cooking over the coals. "And" – he leaned closer, winking at her – "*shrab*, also, courtesy of our Ifren friends."

Dahiya rolled her eyes. "I don't know how you stomach it," she said, eyeing the guerba he held up with misgiving. The spirit made from fermented dates was fiery and harsh. Dahiya held up her own guerba.

"Water," she said, smiling sweetly at Igider. "It tastes better, and it doesn't have the unfortunate effect of making men such as you appear attractive."

The men around them guffawed – all but Zdan, who was watching the sky, frowning.

"Tabat," he said, calling to where Dahiya's father was mending rope. "I do not like the sky."

Tabat grunted. "Perhaps there will be a storm," he said. "Our camp is high enough above the water to remain clear if rain should fall."

"No." Zdan was insistent. "There is something wrong. A storm does not look like that –"

But before he could finish speaking, a strange sound shook the air. It began as a vibration, there but barely felt, and grew rapidly. Within a few moments, the air was alive with an angry buzzing, so loud the men drew swords and looked about them in alarm, trying to discern the source of it.

"Quickly!" Tabat gestured to the camels. "Tie them down!" As men rushed to do his bidding, Dahiya bent to the fire, wrapping the half-cooked birds to save them. She had barely covered one when the purple cloud she had seen earlier descended upon them, and she realised it was not a storm, but rather a cloud of insects, so thick they filled her eyes and ears, crawling into her nose, biting and stinging every piece of her skin.

Startled, she almost dropped the birds, then realised they would need them later. She forced herself to keep hold of them and tried to ignore the high-pitched whirring of the mosquitoes, stumbling toward the saddles where men were already taking refuge under camel blankets, hiding miserably from the sudden attack.

The sound was so deafening that Dahiya may not have noticed the other noise behind her had it not been for Zdan's startled cry. She looked up and saw dawning horror on his face, and even as she turned, she heard her father roar and felt rather than heard Ahar rasp from the scabbard.

The men were veiled, their faces hidden, and they leaped from the cliffs as if they came from the air itself. There were too many to count, seasoned warriors who landed amongst the Jerawa men with drawn swords and bloodcurdling screams. From high on the clifftops came the whistling sound of arrows. Even as Dahiya dropped the birds in her hands and ran for her bow, she saw two of her father's men felled as the arrows struck home.

Tabat was roaring his battle fury, Ahar glinting dully in the purple light as her father cut through insect and flesh, dropping two attackers to the ground with one stroke and whirling to meet another, the clouds of insects parting in an angry whine before rejoining to attack once more. Dahiya crouched behind the camel saddles and drew arrow after arrow, sending them into the midst of the battle, aiming carefully and dropping a man with each draw. She did not think as she pulled the string again and again. Every fibre of her being was focused in her hand, the steadiness of her arm as she breathed in and out, draw and release, allowing the wood to fly in the moment of stillness between the two, the long years of training amongst her father's men cutting through the cloud of insects and wild terror to find her targets.

"Dahiya!"

Her father's cry cut through the odd fog that had fallen across her mind. Dahiya swung to face him, her arrow flying aimlessly into the air.

"*Run*." Tabat mouthed the word, his face twisted with battle rage. A man came at him and he batted him away with a clenched fist, his eyes flashing as they found hers again.

"Go!" he shouted, when she didn't move. "*Go*, Dahiya!"

She scrambled to obey him, stumbling across the ground to where the camels were tied, but she was too late.

Hands grasped at her, and the last thing Dahiya saw, before her body crashed to the ground and darkness fell, was her father's sword falling from his hand as blood-soaked steel protruded from his chest and life left his eyes.

4

WAR

*You, who have been born to peace, do not know what it is to be alone in war.
Whilst our parents live we are still children, even though we may be grown and
fight at their side. But when they are taken, and one must walk this earth with no
more than memory as comfort, then war seems easy by comparison, for what is
the prospect of death, when all that is life is gone?*

The Lady of Aurariola, to her granddaughters
Al Andalus, AD 752

Dahiya woke to the taste of blood in her mouth and the
sound of drunken revelry on the air. From where she lay
on the ground, she could see flames flickering, and smell
roasting meat. The scent turned her stomach. For a moment, she
could not remember why. Then she saw her father's dead face in her
mind and realised that cord bound her hands and feet, whilst a gag
covered her mouth.

She struggled against the ties, crying out behind the cloth. No one
answered. Turning her head to the other side, she saw Zdan and Igider
lying side by side, several feet from her. They were both breathing, she

saw with relief, but neither was awake. She searched the ground for her father, even though she knew it was futile. Tabat was not there. None of the Jerawa men were. Only they three remained, and Dahiya knew in her heart that the rest of her father's Riders were dead.

She swallowed the taste of death, trying to calm the panic in her throat. Her father was no more. She had seen the steel come through his chest herself. Dahiya had not ridden so long amongst warriors without seeing men die. She knew none could survive such a wound.

She inched her body around to the fire, searching the faces there. Her eyes came to rest on one. The man was laughing as he raised his wine flask and drank deeply, the red liquid spilling over his face.

Yedder, thought Dahiya, feeling white rage, liquid in her veins. Her eyes travelled over the faces of his companions, seeing the similarity in their features, the flat jaws and high brows. *They are all Ifren,* she thought. *This attack was no accident. They saw us helpless in the insect storm and seized their chance.*

The Ifren had long coveted the rich valleys of her father's lands, the wealth and status of the Jerawa. To conquer Tabat would give them the right to command the Jerawa – and to take wives from amongst their women.

As if drawn by her thoughts, Yedder looked up, staring straight at her. A slow smile broke on his face.

"The amgar's daughter awakens," he said lightly, and the men around him turned to look at her.

Dahiya wondered that she had not previously noticed the sly cast of his face, the insinuating manner in which he stared at her. She had been so absorbed in thoughts of Apsimar, and the ride ahead to meet him, that she had barely noticed the Ifren man when he had joined them. Now she saw the knowing look in his eyes, the cruel turn of his lips, and fear twisted her belly.

"I could untie you," Yedder said, smiling unpleasantly. "But you have proven lethal with bow and arrow. I'm afraid I must confess that I do not trust you."

His eyes shifted to where Zdan and Igider stirred beside her.

"Ah. And now your two companions also awaken." He smiled at her again. "My men wanted to kill them, as we did your father. But I wish to meet with Ilyan, as your father planned, and unfortunately it is the Jerawa with whom Ilyan has made alliance – not the Ifren." A shadow of anger crossed his face. "The Ifren," he said, "do not meet Count Ilyan's lofty standards, it seems."

"That," spat Igider, who had managed to free his mouth of the gag, "is because the Ifren are liars, cheats, and thieves – a reputation you have proven today."

Yedder's smile faded. "Fine words," he snapped, "from a man I recently spared from death."

"Then kill me," said Igider. "Better that than forced to do your foul work."

"No. I think not." Yedder's smile had returned, cold and flat as stone. "That would deprive me of the pleasure of taking the daughter of your amgar to bride, whilst you watch it happen."

Igider glanced at Dahiya, and the contempt on his face faded, replaced by horror.

"Even you," he said, in a voice that lacked conviction, "would not commit such a crime."

"Men of the Ifren," said Yedder lazily, "have already taken the adwwar of the Jerawa women. By now, their bodies will be ours. Your old people will be dead, the young boys enslaved or killed, the young girls ravaged or dead. Your amgar's gold will adorn the necks of our warriors. Only one thing remains to ensure our victory is complete: to make a marriage with the daughter of the amgar himself."

His eyes, black and foul, rested on Dahiya. "Ilyan is a wealthy man," he murmured. "He seeks to make alliance amongst the Amazigh. He has coin to spare, and he looks for the right man to give it to. You, the daughter of Tabat, will convince him I am that man. And *you*" – he glared at Igider and Zdan – "will testify that you saw the marriage happen, and take me as your amgar."

Choking Igider's strangled protests with a tighter gag, he nodded at one of his men, who came over and loosened Dahiya's, pushing her so she sat up.

"Why would I agree to such a thing?" Dahiya was proud that her voice did not shake.

"Because," said Yedder coldly, "if you do not, I will allow every man at this fire to take you, one after another, whilst the two men beside you watch. And then I will return to your adwwar – with you at my side – and slaughter every man, woman, and child I find there."

Igider and Zdan struggled impotently beside her. Igider's screamed insults were muffled behind the gag. Zdan stared across the fire at Yedder, murder in his quiet eyes. His sisters were in the adwwar, his mother too. Zdan's father was an invalid of an old battle.

He would have fought, Dahiya thought, remembering the old man's quiet dignity. *And he will be dead now.*

Looking at Zdan, she knew he was thinking the same thing.

"And if I agree to marry you?" she said, holding her head high.

Yedder shrugged. "Then we will marry correctly, with women of my adwwar to attend you, and the proper ceremony." He gave her a sly smile. "I will even dance for you," he said, "so you may choose me."

Zdan looked at her, agony in his face. He worked his mouth free of the cloth over it. "Do not do this," he said hoarsely. "Do not give him what he wants."

If it had been a matter of her body alone, Dahiya would have agreed with Zdan and let the men have her whatever way they wished. But in her mind, she saw the small, fragile body of Zdan's youngest sister, a beautiful child no more than eight years old. She imagined the men around the fire taking that small body and violating it in the way she knew Yedder was more than capable of doing, passing her around until there was nothing left but blood and tears.

She drew a deep breath and stared straight at him.

"I agree," she said.

When Yedder stood, Dahiya saw Ahar, her father's sword, hanging at his belt. The jewelled nail that held the leather flap closed was smeared with blood.

5

MARRIAGE

You rarely hear me speak well of the Goths. What praise I have I give to their rule of law, for the Goths were lovers of laws, and they made many. The best of their laws pertained to marriage. Goths understood that, whilst a woman must always be traded on the marriage bed, laws should safeguard her place upon it. The Imazighen have their own laws — and the women of the desert, their own means of enforcing them.

The Lady of Aurariola, to her granddaughters
Al Andalus, AD 752

The adwwar of the Ifren lay below a rocky gulch, on a small, barren plain.

"They have grazed it dry," muttered Zdan as they rode in, their hands bound behind them.

Amazigh did not graze their animals close to the adwwar, just as they did not camp within sight of a well. Some resources were common and belonged to no man. It was the responsibility of the individual to seek grazing for his animals, away from that upon which his clan relied to grow what small crops they could coax from

29

the barren land. To graze so close to the adwwar indicated lazy management.

No mud wall surrounded the adwwar, nor even a thorn-bush fence. The dwellings were low shelters made of tattered hemp and hessian, hung over untrimmed branches. The women were thin and tired, their children listless. What few animals there were had sunken flanks and lowered heads. Dahiya could not help contrasting the mean settlement with the lush, well-kept surrounds of her father's adwwar.

The Ifren emerged from their tents as Yedder led Dahiya into their midst, bound to a camel. She was brought to a halt in the middle of the small plain. The Ifren stood in a silent circle, staring at her.

Yedder waited until they were all present. He drew Ahar from her father's scabbard and thrust it into the air.

"The Jerawa are defeated!" he called. "I have the sword of Tabat in my hand – and tonight, I will have his daughter in my bed!"

The Ifren raised a thin cry.

They are tired, Dahiya thought, looking at the pinched faces and quiet infants. *They are tired and they are hungry. They do not care what sword Yedder holds, nor who shares his bed; they want food for their children and grazing for their animals.*

"Tonight," Yedder went on, "I will slaughter two camels to celebrate our victory. And tomorrow, we will leave this place and take the rich lands of the Jerawa for our home."

This time, the cry they gave was genuine. Camel meat was a rare luxury amongst a people who prized camel flesh above all else. Watching the faces of the Ifren, though, Dahiya could not help but notice their lack of enthusiasm when their eyes turned to their leader.

They do not trust Yedder, she thought.

Yedder had clearly split his force in order to take the Jerawa adwwar at the same time as he took Tabat and his warriors. The Jerawa men had taken two Ifren for every one of their own – perhaps more. With half of their kel far away at the adwwar of the Jerawa, there were less than a dozen men guarding them now, and most bore hard wounds. They obeyed Yedder's orders with the sullen reluctance of men who had invested their faith in the wrong man and were only now beginning to realise their mistake. The wails of grief she heard from the low dwellings around the plain told her that for the women, Yedder's victories had come at a high price.

As the afternoon fell, Dahiya silently submitted to the ministrations of the young women Yedder sent to tend her. They stripped her down and washed her, plucking the hair from her body, and painted henna patterns on her hands and feet. The women clapped and sang in imitation of a true wedding preparation, but their song had a hollow sound, and none of them could meet Dahiya's eyes.

Dahiya ignored them. She gave them her hands for the henna patterns and spread her legs for them to pull her most private hair. She did not flinch and nor did she smile.

Dahiya was thinking.

When night fell, the women draped her in thin indigo cloth, covering her face and body, and placed a chain upon her forehead from which hung a rich, red ruby. Dahiya recognised the jewel. It had once belonged to her mother. Her father never travelled without it.

They led her from the women's tent to the centre of the adwwar where a large fire formed the centre of the gathering. Women took coals from it to the cooking fires behind the crowd, from which the scent of roasting meat rose. Dahiya felt her stomach turn. The stench reminded her of her father, of death.

The women of the Ifren began the slow, rhythmic clapping and yearning song of courtship. Their voices were layered, some ululating whilst others maintained a low, steady beat. An older woman, full bodied with a deeply lined face, sang the lead melody, her voice rising above the others as she sang of the desert night and the ghosts that whispered there, of love, and of veiled men who rode through the sands.

Dahiya felt the song as her own, for she was Amazigh, and the Ifren sang for them all. She heard the song and felt the blood of her father in her veins.

The men of the Ifren emerged from the darkness opposite,

dancing one by one into the flickering light. Their faces were veiled. Indigo powder shaded the skin above and below the eyes, kohl lining them so only the whites showed, gleaming in the darkness. Their robes were wide from their bodies as they spun in the dance, whirling and leaping before her.

In other times, this was the tradition during which women selected their men, chose their marriage partners when the kels came together. Tonight was a sick parody, a macabre puppetry dancing at the command of a weak leader. It was an attempt to legitimise the murder of an ally and the rape of his daughter.

Dahiya watched silently from behind her veil.

The song finally ended, and Yedder stood before her. She inclined her head once in consent. The women shrieked, and Yedder thrust his arms into the air. *As if I had truly chosen him,* Dahiya thought contemptuously. *This is the story he intends to make truth – that I was seduced by his strength. He, the man who slaughtered my father before my eyes.*

Still she sat, welcoming the shield of her veil. Zdan and Igider sat opposite her, their heads down. She felt their shame but did not despise them for it. They were just men, and they could not do what she could.

Dahiya ignored the meat and wine. She sat as a statue whilst the revelry grew raucous, breathing deeply, in and out, the same rhythm with which she had shot her arrows at the Ifren when they took the men of her kel.

Finally, the night grew late, and Yedder stood before her.

"Come, wife," he said, extending his hand. "It is time to take you to my bed."

6

TRESPASS

Women of the Goths believe there is no worse torture a woman can endure than to be ravaged against her will. Women of the Amazigh do not believe thus. A woman's body is her own, renewed by water and at every turn of the moon. No man can possess it; he can merely trespass upon sacred ground for a time, until the woman should reclaim it once more.

The Lady of Aurariola, to her granddaughters
Al Andalus, AD 752

The hemp folds of the tent closed behind them. The women standing barely ten paces from the tent continued their clapping and song, as they would until the work of this night was done.

Yedder approached her, eyes glittering. Taking Ahar from its scabbard, he placed the tip of it at Dahiya's groin, watching her face.

She did not flinch.

"You are quiet," he grunted, his smile oily and wet. "But I will make you scream."

Dahiya did not move, did not speak.

With a sudden gesture, he pulled the sword upward, rending the indigo cloth and the shift beneath it so the material parted neatly on the blade and slid to the floor, leaving only her face covered. His smile widened as his eyes roamed over the tawny swell of her body, resting on the dusky nipples, hard in the cold night air, and the bare cleft between her legs. He put the tip of the sword beneath the veil on her face and lifted it so only the ruby chain held it in place over the unbound hair that hung in ripples to her waist.

"Your father," said Yedder, "was going to give you to Ilyan. Now it is Ilyan who must look upon you and know it is I, the man he disdained, who takes your body as I choose. I, Yedder, who has conquered the Jerawa."

He touched the siyala on her chin with Ahar's cold steel tip. "These seeds," he murmured, "will be Ifren children."

Dahiya held his eyes but did not speak. She felt Ahar's steel on her face like the blood of her father in her veins, and she was not afraid.

Yedder reached out with one rough hand and caught the weight of her breast in it, clutching it convulsively; he groaned, wrenching his robes over his head.

"Look," he grunted, stroking the organ in front of him with coarse eagerness. "No Jerawa man could give you this, could be as hard as I am now. You will feel my sword in your belly tonight."

He thrust his hand between her legs and then, when she didn't respond, knocked her behind the knees with his foot and pushed her down into the blankets. In the corner, myrrh burned on a brazier, and the sickly smoke wafted over Dahiya's face. She inhaled, keeping her eyes open, watching Yedder's face.

"Open your mouth," he muttered, thrusting his tongue between her lips. "I want to kiss you."

He tasted of meat and date wine, smelled of old sweat and the musk he had rubbed on his skin.

"Ah," he groaned, seemingly oblivious to her silence. He thrust two fingers inside her with a hard, jabbing motion and felt the thin barrier of her womanhood between them.

He clambered up her body and clamped his mouth to her

breast, snorting as he sucked at her flesh and groped between her legs. Dahiya stared at him, meeting his eyes when he looked at her, absorbing every moment of the glazed lust she saw in them with cold detachment. He pushed himself up between her legs, panting as he reached down to place himself inside her.

Dahiya did not shrink from his assault. She rose her hips to meet his, taking him inside her unflinchingly. When he tore through and sheathed himself completely, she made no sound but moved with him, so he became enflamed with the feel of her, crying her name hoarsely into the night as he plunged and pillaged her flesh.

It did not last long.

He gave a long, drawn-out cry that ended in a choking, gargled sound, and slumped across her, his seed trickling down her leg.

Dahiya lay motionless beneath him.

Finally, he pushed himself up and looked down at her with a sneering, triumphant smile.

"In the end," he said, pushing her off the blankets, "it is just another hole, even if it is a tight one." He pulled the white cloth from beneath them and stalked to the opening of the tent. Pulling the material aside, he exposed Dahiya's naked body to the eyes of the watching women as he held up the white cloth, the red stain upon it clear and unmistakable in the flickering light of the fire.

The women shrieked and the men cheered, though there was a hollow sound to their voices.

"The Jerawa whore is mine," Yedder shouted, waving the cloth. "Reaved and riven."

He let the cloth fall and turned back to stare at her naked body, still and silent on the blankets.

"I will take you again," he said, rising already at the sight of her, kneeling on the bed and jamming his fingers inside her. "I will take you until you forget your own name."

Dahiya remained prone beneath him and felt every motion.

* * *

IN THE STILL HOURS, Dahiya lay with her eyes open, hearing the steady breath of the man beside her. Yedder had fulfilled his promise. He had taken her until she was raw and bloody and his own member could no longer rise. Then he had slapped her, laughed at her silence, and fallen asleep.

That had been many long moments since, but Dahiya had waited. She wanted to be sure.

She eased her body from beneath him. The tent was dark and the adwwar silent. The revelry had ceased before Yedder himself had; not even camel meat, Dahiya suspected, could enjoin the Ifren to celebration when so many of them had died earning it.

She drew on the robes Yedder had earlier discarded and took his dagger. Her mother's ruby she wore against her head, wrapping Yedder's tagelmust around it. The torn remains of her indigo wedding garb lay in a pile on the floor. She did not look at them.

With steady hands, she buckled Ahar at her side, careful to make no sound. She pulled the jewelled nail from the leather flap on the scabbard, still smeared with her father's blood. Then she came to the bed and stared down at the man lying upon it. Slowly, with cold precision, she put the cold steel of Yedder's dagger beneath his balls, her knee on his throat, and her hand over his mouth, the nail piercing his lips, so her father's blood mingled with his own.

The moment his eyes flew open, she pricked the skin beneath his balls with the dagger and pressed her knee hard into his throat, watching with savage satisfaction as his eyes widened and began to fill with blood.

"You will die now," she whispered against his ear, pressing the dagger higher and her knee deeper. "You will die with your balls on your neck and the meat with which you took me in your own mouth, the blood of my father and of my maidenhead on your tongue. This is how men will remember Yedder of the Ifren – as the man who died choking on a virgin's blood."

With a deft slice, she took his balls, holding the bloody sacks up to his face as his screams were choked in his throat before they could find breath. Carefully, she placed them above her knee, so they sat like a cluster of large grapes on his neck, dripping their juice onto his skin. Another slice of the knife and she held his organ in her hand. Yedder stared at her, abject terror and mindless pain tinged with something else, something that gave Dahiya more delight than the meat in her hands: defeat.

"Open your mouth," she whispered, her face close to his. "I want to kiss you."

With her thumb she forced his jaw wide, and slowly, inch by inch, she fed Yedder his own organ, pushing it down into his gullet until his eyes bulged and the air stopped in his throat. Dahiya stayed there, her knee on his throat, holding the blood-soaked tool until she saw the last light of life fade from the man's eyes.

Then she plunged his knife into his throat below his balls and embedded the jewelled nail deep between his eyes, in the place where his spirit would try to leave his body. She left him there, pinned to the bed, his eyes wide open and terrified in death.

She washed her hands in the water of her guerba and glanced down at Ahar. She would not taint the blade of her father's sword with the blood of the coward who had killed him.

Dahiya of the Jerawa slipped from the tent, veiled and silent as the night, leaving her father's murderer, reaved and riven, on the blankets of her lost innocence.

* * *

DAHIYA MOVED SILENTLY through the adwwar, staying in the shadows. She walked with a wide, confident stride, her hand on Ahar's hilt, straight to the low dwelling at the far end of the camp outside which two men stood guard.

Fools, she thought scornfully, *to show so clearly where you hide your prisoners.*

She was barely three paces from the men before one of them realised something was wrong. He made a guttural noise, but Dahiya had already thrown the knife, which caught him in the throat, and had taken the other with the arrow she held in her hand. Kicking their bodies inside the tent, she moved to where Zdan and Igider lay and untied them, holding a finger to her lips.

"Yedder is dead," she murmured.

"I will get the camels." Igider was scrambling to his feet.

"No."

37

The two men stared at her.

"The Ifren are mine," said Dahiya.

"We will come back to kill them." Zdan put his hand on her arm. "We cannot do this now."

Dahiya shook his hand off. "You will do as I say," she said quietly. She glanced between them. "Or you will die here," she said, and whatever the Jerawa men saw in her face was enough to silence them.

Swiftly they moved through the camp, taking the men one by one, tying and gagging them, but killing none. When it was done, each man lay in a tent alone, bound and gagged, tied tighter than any wild camel could be.

Dahiya gathered the women in the centre of the adwwar, by the dying fire.

"Your men chose a fool for a leader," she said. "Yedder is dead, lying in the bed upon which he thought to take me, his own manhood bloody in his throat. I am Dahiya, daughter of Tabat of the Jerawa, and no man takes what I do not choose to give."

The women stared back at her, their faces tired and afraid.

"I have not killed your men," Dahiya said, "though I found them dull with drink and exhaustion and could have taken them all. I do not kill them because to do so would condemn you, also, to death. I choose instead to give you life – and a choice."

They looked up at that.

"Soon, I and my men will ride from here," Dahiya said. "We will take what we need, and no more. We ride for Carthage as my father intended, to meet with Ilyan and join war against the Arabs who dare come upon our land.

"For that fight, we need men. Those of the Ifren that remain alive; those of every tribe of the Amazigh. Men to fight for the land that is ours and for the people we are together. I will not take more men from that fight, not even those who have shed the blood of my own father.

"I will return here, after I meet with Ilyan. I will bring men – many of them. When I do, your men may join us. If they are gone from this place, they will be my enemy. If your men do not join mine, you, too, will be my enemy."

She paused and looked around at the waiting faces.

"If you unbind your men before the end of tomorrow," she said, "or if any of them follow us, I will return here and kill every man, woman, and child. If I am dead before I can do so, my spirit will poison every waterhole at which you halt, and take every infant born to you. No veil will hold my ghost at bay. No invocation will shield the souls of your children. Wrong was done me; wrong I do not count if it brings your people to our cause – but, make no mistake, wrong I will see righted if you dare cross me, now or ever again, in this world or the next."

She looked amongst them until she found the old woman who had sung the wedding song the night before.

"You," she said, beckoning her forward. "Will you keep the men bound, and your word to this promise?"

The old woman did not pause. "We are yours," she said, her voice strong and clear. "The swords of the Ifren belong to you, Dahiya."

Dahiya nodded, unsmiling.

"Good," she said, standing to leave.

"Amgar."

Dahiya turned, startled at the title.

The old woman held out her hand in invitation.

Dahiya paused for a moment, then lowered her head. The old woman placed her hand on it in the traditional gesture of blessing.

"May your grief be your power," she said softly.

Dahiya stood and stepped back, letting the hand slide away. She hit her chest once, holding her clenched fist across her heart, her eyes taking in each face before her.

Then she gestured to Zdan and Igider, who watched her with wary eyes.

"Come," she said. "We have far to ride."

* * *

By DAWN they had left the Ifren far behind, and a day later Dahiya knew they had not been followed.

She had not washed, and nor had she paused to rest. She could

39

feel Yedder's seed dry and tight on her skin, taste his sweat and stench on her tongue and in his robes. She let it stay there, on her body, in her nostrils. Dahiya would not forget Yedder.

She would never forget.

The pads of her camel moved across the desert floor and their silent rhythm beat the woman's words in her mind: *May your grief be your power be your grief be your power be your grief…*

She wondered what power could be left to her when her father and his Riders were dead. Tabat's death sat within her in a way her mother's never had, even before she had taken her revenge and set the ghost of her pain free. Her grief for Tabat was different. It clawed at her innards, corroding the fibres of her being until she thought the pain of it might drive her mad. She longed for her father like a starving man watched food just beyond his reach. Every question she had never asked him, every rough touch she had lightly received, choked her throat with anger and pain. Dahiya thought she could endure Yedder's abuse upon her body a thousand times if she could only ask her father once more what he thought she should do, what course she should take.

She rode through another night numb and empty within, feeling the fluids of Yedder's body mingle with hers on her skin, until they reached an oasis where there were no men camped and Zdan and Igider fell from their camels with exhaustion. Then she rested.

In the afternoon, she walked away from their sleeping forms and lowered her body into the warm water, just as she had done only days earlier, when she had still been Dahiya, daughter of Tabat, a child playing at life.

She submerged herself in the water and watched the day disappear from view. Under the surface, she felt her heart beat a slow drum and the old woman's words thud in her chest: *May your grief be your power be your grief be your power be your grief…*

The words grew in her chest and became a ball of heat that threatened to fill her body, thudding through her veins with power and life, taking the wrong done to her and making of it a weapon harder than her father's steel, more lethal than any arrow she could draw – a force so primal and rich it spread through her being and became part of her until Dahiya could no longer discern the words from the beating of her own heart.

May your grief be your power.

It was Tabat's voice she heard, loud within her, and she knew then that her father's spirit had not travelled beyond the sands but had instead gone into the water to become part of his daughter, flowing through her veins so he might never be lost to her, lending Dahiya the power that had been his and which now, she knew, must be hers to wield.

She burst to the surface and gasped air into her chest, feeling savage triumph thrill through her body.

I am Dahiya, Amgar of the Jerawa.

* * *

"WE SHOULD RIDE to our own people," said Igider the next morning as they saddled the camels.

"We ride for Carthage."

"But our people —"

"What would you do, Igider?" Dahiya cut through his words without facing him. "Would you ride with three of us — you and Zdan both wounded — to retake our adwwar? What use would that be?"

"We took the Ifren," said Igider stubbornly.

"The Ifren were drunk and tired, their amgar dead. We took nothing but broken, sleeping men. By now, the men who took our adwwar know their own is conquered. If we return now, we are no more than corpses."

"She is right." Zdan spoke quietly from her other side.

Igider made a derisive noise.

"You can name me coward if you wish," Zdan said. "My sisters were in the adwwar the Ifren took. My mother." He swallowed. "My father," he said quietly, "will be dead by now. Do not think I lack your desire for vengeance, Igider."

"Then ride with me," said Igider roughly. He turned to Dahiya. "I know you have suffered," he said. "That you may, even now, bear

41

Yedder's child in your belly. I will marry you anyway. None need ever know of your shame."

Dahiya's hands stilled on the ropes. She met his eyes. "I will tell the whole world," she said softly. "Not of my shame, Igider, for I have none, but of the vengeance I took. And any child I bear will be a warrior, the seed of Tabat" – she touched the siyala on her chin – "no matter who brings him forth from my body."

"You must marry." Igider's face was red. "You must allow one of us to stand forth as amgar of the Jerawa. You cannot bear your father's sword –"

Dahiya moved swiftly. Ahar flashed in her hand and lay beneath Igider's throat. "I carry my father's power, Igider, and I carry his blood. His sword is my arm."

She held his eyes, her hands steady. "I lead the Jerawa now. If you do not choose to follow me, ride where you will. I am for Carthage – and Ilyan."

"And Apsimar," hissed Igider. "You ride for the golden-haired commander, Dahiya, and no one else."

He winced as Ahar drew a thin line of blood on his chin, then Dahiya whirled away from him and mounted her camel.

"I ride for Altava," she said, as the camel rose. "For the land my father fought for. You" – she turned away from him – "you are Amazigh, Igider, and free to choose your own path."

She did not turn back to look behind her, but when they made camp many miles later, Igider was with them.

7

LEGEND

Carthage, modern day Tunisia

*The things that made Dahiya legend are never sung of. They are whispered.
Goths cross themselves when they tell such stories. Arabs spit to the ground and
look around warily, for they at least know of the desert spirits they call djinn.
Men say Dahiya killed her father's murderer with a nail. They do not speak the
truth, for to do so would be to admit to fears no man wishes to contemplate.*

The Lady of Aurariola to her granddaughters
Al Andalus, AD 752

They left their camels on the plains beyond Carthage, in the
care of men paid to graze them. If the men she paid
thought it odd that Dahiya wore the robes of a man and a
weapon of war, they did not speak of it. They were men of
Carthage and had seen stranger sights than a woman bearing a
sword.

Dahiya entered the city at sunset, flanked by Zdan and Igider, her face well veiled. None cast her more than a cursory look. Her robes, though washed free of Yedder's stench, were tired from the journey, and they all three were thin from the ride. They were simply three more nomads in a city teeming with every manner of life.

They entered through a gate set into a solid stone block wall five feet thick and standing high enough that the men atop it were barely visible. Inside the gate was another earthen defence, backed by a second wall, thicker and higher again.

"I have never seen a place so fortified," murmured Zdan; the walls ran the landward length of the city, joining at the sea wall on either end.

"I have never seen a place like it at all," said Igider, staring about him in wonder.

Men wheeling wagons laden with scented herbs called to the donkeys pulling them. Merchants cried their wares in the streets; even the water sellers were garish, dressed in brilliant colours and touting their gourds and cups.

The great piazza, of such size and scale that it boasted a temple and offices at the centre, was a seething mass of people. A busy grid of streets ran about the old circus, all pointing traffic down toward the centre of Carthage – the twin ports.

The circular port was where they were headed. Built inside the city walls, it was where the Greek fleet kept its dromons. The seaward port was the domain of the merchants, lined with huge, vaulted buildings, housing craftsmen of every persuasion.

After the clear air of the desert, the pungent stench of Carthage hit Dahiya in a wall of sensory attack: sea water, cooking meat, human and animal waste, nuts roasting on coals. They passed a Christian church and myrrh-scented smoke wafted across her face, recalling her ill-fated wedding night, the feeling of Yedder's body above her. She inhaled deeply, suppressed a shudder, and walked on through it.

Guards halted them at the entrance to the circular harbour, which lay beneath a great stone gateway. One pushed Dahiya with his *kontarion*, the long, steel-tipped spear with which the Greek soldiers were armed.

"You do not pass here," he said rudely, eyeing their desert garb, the dark eyes amidst indigo cloth.

Dahiya shrugged the coils of cloth from her head, exposing her face, her unbound hair, and the large ruby that hung over her forehead. The guard lowered his spear and stared at her in surprise.

"Tell your commander that Dahiya of the Jerawa is come to see him," she said.

The great circular harbour had an entirely different atmosphere to the seaward merchant port. Barely a man here was out of uniform, and the harbour was ordered, tidy, and a hive of efficient activity. Some dromons were pulled up out of the water for repairs. Others were being washed down and repaired where they lay. All had men coming and going busily. On Dahiya's entrance to the port, however, men stopped in their tasks and stared in open-mouthed amazement at the young girl who strode so confidently across the ground, hair cascading down her back, the last of the dying sun silhouetting the shape of her body beneath the robes as she followed the guard into the tall building at the end of the dock.

It was not Apsimar who met her, but a younger man, dressed in desert robes as she was. He was as tall as her father had been and bore a sword the length of Ahar. He greeted her courteously with the long, patient queries of the Amazigh, looking respectfully away as he did so. Only when they were at an end did he gesture to the *lectus* opposite. Dahiya eyed it warily. She was unaccustomed to sitting on anything other than cushions on sand, and she waited for the man to assume a lounging position before she herself followed suit, Zdan and Igider equally uneasy on either side of her.

"I was expecting Apsimar and Ilyan," she said.

The man inclined his head. "I am Aksil," he said, "of the Awraba – though Apsimar and the Greeks call me Cæcilius. I command Apsimar's men in the interior."

Dahiya lifted her eyebrows. "You command Greek troops?"

"And those Amazigh who fight with them." He looked at her curiously. "I was told to expect your father, Tabat."

"Where is Apsimar?"

Aksil's eyes narrowed. "One might instead ask," he said evenly, "where your father is."

Dahiya returned his stare without speaking.

He waited, his face growing less friendly as the moments stretched out. Finally: "Apsimar and Ilyan were summoned back to Septem," he said tightly.

"Summoned? By whom?"

Aksil beckoned to the door and a tall man with dark, hooded eyes entered. His eyes slid over her body unpleasantly, and there was a sly cast to his face that made Dahiya's hand tighten on Ahar's hilt.

"Giscila is a Goth, from Spania," Aksil said. He nodded at the man, who stepped forward.

"The King of Spania has died." Giscila licked his lips unpleasantly as he watched her. He spoke in Latin so guttural and heavy that Dahiya could barely make out the words. "My brother, Wamba, now sits beneath the votive crown there – but rebellion threatens. Ilyan's port is barely a day from Spania's shores. My brother fears our enemies may retreat to Septem, possibly even take the port itself."

"Apsimar's orders from Constantinople," Aksil cut in, "are that Septem must be held, at any cost. He and Ilyan sailed there immediately, with twenty of Apsimar's dromons."

"And yet you remain here," said Dahiya to Giscila. "Why?"

Giscila's face grew pinched and ugly. "What I do," he spat, "is no business of yours. I am the brother of a king."

His crude, boastful response was so unlike the calm humility of the Amazigh that Dahiya could do nothing but stare at him; in another place and time, he would have died for such insult. Instead, Dahiya turned to Aksil, who had the grace at least to look uncomfortable.

"Apsimar left you here – in command of the fleet?" Dahiya did not attempt to hide her scepticism. She had not been raised Tabat's daughter without knowing something of the imperial forces and their power.

"No." Aksil frowned at her. "He left me here to meet your father. And so I must ask again – why does Tabat send his daughter in his stead, when he promised both men and iron to our cause?"

"My father is dead," said Dahiya flatly. "He was killed when we were attacked by the Ifren."

Aksil paled.

"We were taken captive," Dahiya said in answer to his unspoken question. "We escaped."

"And the Ifren? The Jerawa?"

"Our adwwar remains in Ifren hands."

Dahiya felt Zdan and Igider shift uncomfortably beside her, but she said nothing of Yedder or her ill-fated wedding. There was no reason for this Aksil to know any more than she chose to tell him.

"The Awraba are allied to the Jerawa," she said. "We ask your support, as amgar, to take back our adwwar. In return you will have our swords, as my father promised."

Aksil's mouth twisted sceptically.

"And you speak for the Jerawa?" His eyes shifted to the men either side of her. "You," he addressed them, "follow this child as your amgar?"

There was a long silence, during which Dahiya did not move. She would not let them see her uncertainty. Finally, Igider spoke.

"Yes," he said quietly, looking Aksil in the eye. "Without her, we would be dead. Dahiya carries Ahar, her father's sword, and has earned the right to speak for us."

Aksil sat back, not attempting to hide his derision. Beside him, Giscila's face was blatantly contemptuous.

"I will not send my men to follow a girl on a mission of revenge," Aksil said bluntly. "There is an Arabic army at Kairouan, and I am here to hold it at bay. If you have no men to offer our cause, I have no use for you."

"You will not offer us your help?"

Dahiya thought of the women and children of their adwwar, even now at the mercy of the Ifren, and felt a hollowness in her stomach.

"I will not." Aksil's tone was impatient now. He glanced at the men beside her. "If you wish to fight," he said curtly, "you may join the Awraba and be welcome."

Dahiya stood. Keeping her eyes on Aksil, she slowly wrapped the coils of her tagelmust about her face, tucking her hair beneath it, until only her eyes glowed over the indigo wrap.

"Ilyan and my father were allies," she said behind the veil. "If he is in Septem, then that is where I will go."

Aksil stared at her. "Septem is a thousand miles by sea."

Dahiya glanced at the harbour. "And there are a thousand dromons here. One of them at least will be bound there."

"Your battles are here," said Aksil, his voice rising.

Dahiya gave him a hard look. "You just told me," she said softly, "that you will not send men to follow a girl. If that be the case, surely it can be no concern of yours what battles I choose."

Turning to Giscila, she nodded politely. "Brother to a king," she said courteously, "I wish you well."

She had left the port before she dared to look anywhere but directly ahead. She almost sagged with relief when she found Zdan and Igider behind her, particularly when she saw them grinning.

"I thought you would stay," she admitted.

"And I never thought I would see Aksil of the Awraba lost for words," said Igider, unable to hide the admiration in his eyes. "Did you know his name means 'the Leopard'? Men fear him, Dahiya. And you just left the man speechless."

"Not to mention," added Zdan, his eyes shining, "insulted a brother of the Gothic king."

Dahiya lowered her eyes, not wanting to show her pleasure.

"I am going to Septem," she said. "There is nothing for us here. If we are to take back our people, we need Ilyan."

"Then we will go with you," said Zdan quietly.

She looked between them. "Are you certain?"

Igider gave a snort of laughter. "I am. But before we go" – he gestured to one of the taverns that lined the market – "I reserve the right to tell the story of your wedding night to men over wine. If I am to follow a woman, I would have men know what manner of killer she is."

Dahiya was grateful for the veil that hid her face. She shrugged, as if she cared nothing for his words.

"Do what you will," she said lightly. "I will sell a ruby and buy us passage."

By the time they sailed the next morning, all of Carthage knew that Dahiya of the Jerawa had cut the balls from her husband on the night of their wedding and choked him to death on his own cock.

8

———————

SEPTEM

Septem, modern day Ceuta, Morocco

Goths now describe Ilyan's court as if it were a den of sin to rival hell itself and his progeny whores of the devil. They forget he held Septem at a time when the world itself shifted beneath us and all we knew shimmered like a mirage upon the desert, feared lost in every moment. Ilyan was genius and magician – but he was also man, and Dahiya perhaps the only woman who ever truly knew him.

The Lady of Aurariola, to her granddaughters
Al Andalus, AD 752

In the end, Dahiya did not need to sell her ruby to buy them passage to Septem. The price of their camels was more than enough to put them aboard a bireme dromon belonging to a Nabatean merchant who had sailed the Circle of Lands for thirty years and knew how to catch a favourable breeze in the lateen sails. They covered the distance to Septem in little more than the turn of a moon, arriving as midwinter approached.

Dahiya could see the rugged coastline of Spania in the distance as she stepped from the dromon to the dock. She stared at the blue shadow across the water, wondering what kind of land it was that the Goths had united under the crismon-and-peacock banner that fluttered on one of the dromons in the port. She had known little of Goths at all until they had drawn their vessel one night upon a shore beside an entire crew of the tall, blond men who had ruled in Spania for more than three centuries. She could not understand their coarse tongue, and she found their long braids and many jewels an odd affectation for men who carried swords, but she had struck up a conversation in Greek with one man, and it had stayed with her.

Like the Amazigh, the man had told her, his people had once been driven from their homeland, which lay far to the north. They had come to the ancient territories of Hispania as citizens of Rome, then carved an independent nation from the crumbling remains the Empire left behind. The last of the imperial forces had been thrust from their shores less than fifty years ago. Now the Goths had a nation they called Mater Spania, a homeland of their own once more, and they paid tribute to no man.

Dahiya admired that.

A cold wind whipped up from the sea, and Dahiya pulled her camel blanket close about her shoulders as they walked up the paved road toward the imposing palace high on a cliff overlooking the port. Dahiya could have purchased clothes in Carthage more fitting for the amgar of the Jerawa: a cloak of fine wool, perhaps. But she took a perverse pride in the travel-stained desert robes that had once belonged to the man who had tried to make her his wife, just as she took comfort in the familiar scent of camel close to her skin. She could feel the desert close by, and she longed for it. Dahiya was a woman of the sands. She missed her people, and she longed for her land.

The palace was an airy, light structure built when Rome reigned supreme and the finest marble was not spared. Fountains strong with winter rains gushed amidst scented gardens, and the carved pillars that marked the entrance to Ilyan's council were thicker than three men. Dahiya stepped inside the wide, high chamber and glared at the man guarding the heavy wooden doors when she found him staring at her. His eyes dropped to the heavy sword at her side and the men who stood grimly behind her, and he lowered his eyes, chastened.

"Ilyan," she said to the man on the dais. "We must talk."

"Dahiya." Ilyan leaped from the dais, his eyes gleaming with something almost, Dahiya thought, like excitement.

He came down the steps toward her, his hands out. "What an extraordinary – and unexpected – pleasure." His eyes travelled over her robes, the camel blanket across her shoulders. "You will want to bathe, and rest, I am sure. My people will find you clothes –"

"I did not come here for pleasure, Ilyan."

"Ah." Ilyan tilted his head to one side, regarding her, and the light in his eyes faded to the detached, slightly cynical cast she remembered.

"Then," he said politely, "perhaps – wine?" He gestured to the dais. Dahiya stalked ahead of him and sat cross-legged on the floor, sweeping her robes neatly beneath her. Although she felt his eyes upon her, his face when he joined her wore nothing more than bland courtesy.

Zdan and Igider remained at a respectful distance toward the rear of the chamber, staring about them with barely disguised curiosity. Even in Carthage, neither of them had seen such luxury.

"Please ensure my men are fed," Dahiya instructed the servant who brought wine. He stared at her in fascination and backed away from view, casting her curious glances as he went.

Ilyan handed her a carved silver cup. They drank.

"My father," said Dahiya without preamble, "is dead."

Ilyan's eyes narrowed infinitesimally. He drank a measured sip and lowered the cup.

"I am deeply sorry." He inclined his head. "Tabat was a good man and a strong ally."

"As is his daughter." Dahiya held his eyes. "And as such, Ilyan, I have come to ask your help."

"Oh?" Ilyan's face was disinterested, but Dahiya could see the intellectual movement behind the facade, and she found herself, again, liking him.

"The Ifren took our adwwar," she said. "After they killed my father and most of our men."

"You want revenge." Ilyan nodded; Dahiya could tell she had already lost his interest.

"No," she said.

He looked back at her with raised brows. "No?"

"No." Dahiya smiled coldly. "I have already taken my revenge. The man who killed my father is dead, his mouth filled still with the rotting part of himself with which he thought to violate me."

This time, Ilyan's hand actually paused in the act of raising his wine cup.

"Yedder of the Ifren took me to bride," Dahiya continued. "His wedded bliss, however, did not last long."

Ilyan stared at her for a long moment.

Then he sat back, his eyes sparkling, and saluted her with his cup as he drank. "My compliments," he said politely.

Dahiya could not help it. She burst out laughing.

Ilyan looked at her, his eyes bright with humour. "I amuse you?"

"Yes," Dahiya said, still shaking with a laughter that she could not have known she needed. "Oh, Ilyan. My men have told the tale of my wedding night from Carthage to Septem, and each time it is told, men run from me, their faces cowed in fear and superstition. But you" – she shook her head, looking at him with something like admiration – "you raise your wine cup and drink."

"To drink wine," said Ilyan mildly, "I find to be the best course of action in most circumstances. Unless, of course, one is with a woman with whom one intends to lie – in which case moderation is advised."

His eyes caught hers and lingered.

"Am I," he said softly, "in the presence of such a woman, Dahiya of the Jerawa?"

For a moment, Dahiya thought she saw something hard gleam in their depths, then her own mouth twisted in a smile and the moment was gone, Ilyan's detachment returned.

"No, Ilyan," she said, "you are not. Will that alter the outcome of our discussions here?"

"Not at all," murmured Ilyan, seemingly unperturbed by her

rejection. "Although" – he raised one mildly sardonic eyebrow – "I believe we have both missed a marvellous opportunity."

He turned an enquiring eye to Igider and Zdan in the corner. "*Your* men," he mused, repeating her earlier statement. "I take it, then, that you are now amgar in your father's place?"

"I am," said Dahiya simply.

He raised his cup in another silent salute.

"I wish to honour my father's agreement with you." Dahiya leaned forward. In the midwinter light, the marble gleamed palely, reflecting the pale blue of Ilyan's eyes. He watched her, and Dahiya was aware of an odd current between them, a kind of understanding she could not have explained but found both comforting and exhilarating at the same time.

Briefly she explained how she had left things with the Ifren.

"In the desert south of our adwwar," she said, turning the wine cup in her hands, "two thousand more Jerawa wait, scattered in camps throughout the red mountains and the sands. I will bring them all to your cause. They owe allegiance to my father. They will fight for me."

"Why have you not gone to them already, if this is the case?"

"Because I am a girl half the age of their youngest leader." Dahiya met his eyes. "They will take my father's sword and force me to kneel to marry whom they choose." She stood, moving restlessly about the dais. "My father fought for twenty years to lead the heads of the Jerawa clans. From infancy, Ilyan, I rode with him. I know those men. I have sat in council with all of them at my father's fire. I know their weaknesses and their abilities. There is not one of them who is worthy of wearing my father's sword, nor capable of leading our entire kel into battle against the forces you described waiting for us at Kairouan."

"But you," said Ilyan, "believe you possess those abilities?"

"I know I do."

Ilyan sat back and regarded her thoughtfully. "Men will speak to you of strategy. They will ask your plans and deride them when you speak."

"I can manage men, Ilyan."

"I would wish you did not have to."

Ilyan stood abruptly and strode to the window, his robes behind his back, face hidden from her. "I would wish you safely here, Dahiya, and my men leading yours in this war. You do not know what you begin here."

"But you do not doubt me."

"No." There was an odd note in his voice she could not read. "No, Dahiya, I do not doubt you — though men will. Even after you prove yourself a thousand times over, they will."

The light faded and a sea mist fell outside the lattice windows, cloaking the room with a strange, mystical intimacy.

"And what do you ask of me?" Ilyan's voice was low.

"A show of strength." Dahiya did not move. "Send men of the fleet with me to the interior. Let the Jerawa see the blond commander astride a horse, with five hundred men behind him. Let them see those who seek alliance with Tabat's daughter."

"And now we come to it." When he turned to her, Ilyan's eyes glittered with an odd light. "It is Apsimar you want."

Dahiya felt her heart judder in her chest at the name.

"I want no man, Ilyan," she said coldly. "Only the power they represent."

A movement of Ilyan's eyes warned her at the same time as she felt the air move behind her, and she tensed.

"Remind me," came a deep, amused voice from over her shoulder, "not to forget that."

9

DESTINY

Dahiya's legend speaks of her liaison with a Greek commander. His name is never spoken, for the position to which he would rise deters men from idle gossip, on pain of death. But we, who knew him long before he rose to such lofty heights, know the truth — and the truth is that Apsimar and Dahiya were destined as surely as stars in the heavens.

The Lady of Aurariola, to her granddaughters
Al Andalus, AD 752

"I cannot spend so long away from my ships again." Apsimar shook his head and sat back against the wall, long legs crossed before him, arms folded over his chest. Bronze cuffs gleamed on his forearms, and he appeared entirely untroubled by the chill in the room.

As if, Dahiya thought, *he burns inside with his own sun.*

She swallowed and looked away. Apsimar disturbed her, now even more than when they had met previously. He spoke to Ilyan, but his eyes were on her. He sat on a *lectus* by the wall, looking down on them both.

"I can send messages ahead," she said. "Ask that the Jerawa leaders meet us at the old city of Thamugadi, closer to your ships. They will come if they believe it is to meet a commander of the Greek forces."

"Do your people have so much respect, then, for our forces?" Apsimar looked at her quizzically. "History would not suggest it is so."

"They have respect for your coin." Dahiya shrugged. "And they hate the Arabs – more than you do."

Apsimar glanced at Ilyan. "You support this?"

Ilyan's half smile gave nothing away. "They are your men, Apsimar. It is your decision."

Apsimar closed his eyes briefly. His arms were locked tightly together, the muscles beneath the bronze cuffs like iron cord. One hand opened and closed in a convulsive clench. He took a deep breath. When he looked at her again it was with critical scrutiny, his eyes clear and incisive.

"How would you array men against Uqba?"

"Lure the Arab forces from their port," Dahiya answered promptly. "Lead them into the desert, where their horses will flounder and their men grow afraid. Attack them in the nights when the sand blows about them and they do not know where the sun has gone, nor how to find stars to guide their way. Force them to the mountains where my people, mounted on horse instead of camel, wait."

"Uqba has ten thousand men. Your men cannot take them all in the nights."

Dahiya leaned down, one elbow on her knee.

"Harry them to the place you choose," she said softly. "Then force them to battle. Let them come, and come, wave after wave. Let them think they win. And then, when they are tired and beginning to relax in their victory" – she smiled slowly, holding Apsimar's eyes – "unleash our Riders," she said, "on horseback. The desert men who can fire five arrows with one draw and wheel a horse with no hand on the rein."

Apsimar's eyes narrowed. "It is my men who will come at them, wave after wave?"

"It is what they will expect. It is the way the Greeks have fought them before, the way they will expect to be fought again."

"Your people, too, have fought thus. Cæcilius defeated Uqba in pitched battle. He will not like the idea of skulking in the rear whilst a Greek army takes his glory."

"Cæcilius" – Dahiya used the Greek name Aksil had affected with distaste – "will fight with you. He will not wish me near the battlefield, nor near his men." Nor, she thought, would her men like using a name given to their leader by outsiders, in place of one given him at birth in their own tongue.

"And your men?" Apsimar looked at her with hard eyes. "How do you expect them to call you amgar yet follow Cæcilius into battle?"

"They will follow Cæcilius on my orders." She met his eyes in the dim half-light and saw something flare in his, there and then gone. "The Riders are mine, Apsimar. They will come from the rear, when all believe our cause lost."

"You believe you can guarantee this," he said flatly.

"I do." She forced her voice to remain steady. "But I cannot offer you this chance if you do not ride with me now." She swallowed hard on the bitter taste of humiliation in her mouth, keeping her eyes on his. "The Jerawa," she said, and now it was impossible to keep the anger from her voice, "will not follow me alone. Not unless I bring something they do not have."

"Bringing my men to your cause might grant you temporary command." Apsimar's voice was uncompromising. "But it will not be the reason you keep it. Nor will I send good men to their deaths unnecessarily."

In the corner, a slave a lit a torch, and light flared on the hard planes of Apsimar's face.

"Give me command," said Dahiya in a low, furious tone, "and I will never give you cause to regret it."

His mouth twisted. "I do not make decisions that lead to regret. I will give you your men." His arms unfolded, and when he stretched his fingers Dahiya saw half-moons where his nails had dug into his palms. "But if I do not like your leadership," he said flatly,

"I will replace you without thought. Do we understand one another, Dahiya of the Jerawa?"

Dahiya forced her pride into her arm and punched her clenched fist against her left breast, seeing surprise flare briefly in Apsimar's face.

"I understand," she said softly.

He hesitated for a moment, then clenched his own fist, matching her gesture.

For a moment, they stared at each other.

"Very well, then." Apsimar stood decisively. "I will land my ships on the coast to the east and ride south to Thamugadi." He glanced at Ilyan. "And you?"

Ilyan had been watching them with a faint smile, his chin resting on the long, thin fingers.

"I cannot leave my port," he said. "Not whilst Spania is in turmoil. I must await the results of their wrangling and pay my respects to the new king. It does not do to ignore trouble so close to my shores."

"You do not believe Spania would attack Septem?" Apsimar frowned.

"No." Ilyan waved a dismissive hand. "The Goths are absorbed with their northern border and squabbling with the Franks. But for thirty years, Chindasuinth and his sons have ruled. Now Reccesuinth, son of Chindasuinth, is dead, and a man named Wamba sits beneath the crown. I have heard strange tales of his family. I do not yet know quite what manner of man my neighbour across the sea is to be."

Dahiya remembered the man with Aksil, back in Carthage. "I met a man who claims to be brother to the new king," she said.

"You met Giscila?" Ilyan looked at her thoughtfully.

Dahiya nodded. "In Carthage." She made the contemptuous gesture used by the Amazigh to dismiss those not worthy of carrying a sword. "He was not a man."

"When we spoke earlier," Ilyan said, "of your plans to attack the Arabic force, you mentioned horses. Do you have enough horses for your Riders to mount such an attack?"

Puzzled, Dahiya shook her head. "Not yet," she said. "But why ask such a question? Horses can be acquired. And we were speaking of kings."

Ilyan held up a finger. "There is a Spaniard in my port," he said, "who has brought a shipment of the finest horseflesh in all the Circle of Lands. Horseflesh so sought after, in fact, that I could have sold the entire shipment before ever the animals arrived here. However, the person who brought them came seeking Giscila, the very man you met in Carthage, Dahiya. Perhaps, if I introduce you, an arrangement could be made. The Illiberis horses, believe me, are worth it."

Dahiya shrugged. "A horse is a horse," she said. "But if it please you, Ilyan – then yes."

Apsimar was still standing, hands planted firmly on his hips, legs wide as if he straddled the deck of one of his dromons. Dahiya was acutely aware of his nearness, the blue eyes noting her every move.

"Perhaps you would honour me with your company, Dahiya," he said. "We can discuss how we will meet at this Thamugadi and what I must say to these allies of yours."

"Of course." Feigning indifference, Dahiya stood, letting the tagelmust fall to her neck, her hair rippling down her back. She saw his eyes go to it, felt the weight of his gaze on her skin.

"Ilyan," she said. "Perhaps we can talk again tomorrow of horses."

Ilyan waved a careless hand.

"You are both staying within the palace walls," he said, examining a nail with studied interest. "I am certain our paths will cross."

Dahiya felt her skin warm at the thought of Apsimar's body lying abed under the same roof as her own. As if he sensed her thoughts, Apsimar moved closer to her as they made for the tall wooden doors. "An arrangement," he murmured, "unlikely to grant me a deep slumber, I fear."

Not knowing how to reply to that, Dahiya stalked through the doors and made for the gardens, terribly aware of Apsimar's lean height behind her.

She rapidly realised her mistake. Ilyan's gardens had been designed by Romans in a time of lewd gods and carnal appetites. Everywhere she looked were mosaics depicting erotic scenes, wrought in hidden corners designed for intimacy. She walked into one, bound at the end by the overhanging branches of a fig tree, and turned to find Apsimar, arms folded, grinning as he blocked her exit.

"Thamugadi," she said, in a voice that was not quite steady, "will take you five days on horseback from the coast. I will send men to meet you."

Apsimar tilted his head, regarding her with amusement. "Will you not escort me yourself?"

"I will be occupied," she said, pulling a leaf from the tree and tearing it with her fingers. "Gathering those we need for our cause."

"But I do not care about the others." Apsimar stepped closer, lowering his voice. "I come to Thamugadi for you, Dahiya, not them."

She stepped back and felt the cold stone against her skin. In contrast, the lean heat of his body loomed over her, and her voice was slightly breathless when she said: "I was recently married."

Apsimar paused in the act of raising his finger to her face. He frowned. "I was not aware." He glanced over his shoulder. "Is your husband here?"

Dahiya looked at him steadily. "He is dead."

"Dead," Apsimar repeated flatly.

Dahiya nodded. "I killed him," she said. "On our wedding night."

Apsimar regarded her. "Why do you tell me this?" he said finally.

"Because it is a tale men will tell." Dahiya met his eyes. "And I would rather you know it from me." She swallowed and dropped her eyes. "I do not carry his child," she muttered, feeling her face warm.

His hand shot out and grasped her chin, not gently, so she must look up at him. He was looking at her closely. "He hurt you," Apsimar said, and there was no trace of warmth in his voice.

She shook her head free and stared back at him, tilting her chin proudly. "Not as much as I hurt him," she said. "Few men know the pain he did before I brought an end to his life."

Apsimar's mouth tightened. "Good," he said coldly.

He stepped back, and Dahiya felt oddly bereft, though she would not allow him to see it. He turned away so his face was in profile. His smile was gone. She supposed he would not want her now. She knew it was often so, with the Greeks, that they valued only virgin brides, unlike her own people, who knew a woman grew in soul with the life she lived and became of more value, not less, through her trials.

"I, too, am married," he said, without looking at her. "I would not have told you this." He glanced sideways. "And no man would dare speak of it."

Dahiya nodded. "Does she give you children, this wife?"

He seemed surprised by her question. "Yes." He frowned. "I have a daughter – an infant, when I sailed."

"This is good." Dahiya smiled widely at him. "Daughters are the keepers of water," she said. "All men should have daughters. Is she a good wife to you, this woman?"

Apsimar was regarding her with open confusion now. "Yes," he said hesitantly. "She is a woman of honour and of a good family. I respect her."

"I am pleased." Dahiya smiled. "A man such as you needs a wife of honour."

Apsimar shook his head. "It does not concern you," he said, "that I have a wife?"

"Does it concern you," Dahiya countered, "that I put a blade through the man who ravaged me?"

"It concerns me that he hurt you." Apsimar frowned. "But I am glad you took your revenge." He touched her face with one long finger. "Do you carry the hurt within you?" he said, as if struggling to find the words he meant. "Does it – has it changed you?"

Dahiya put her hand over her chest. She could hear her heart thudding with the rhythm she had found in the sands, feel power lick through her, intoxicating and painful at once. She stepped nearer him, so his hand opened to cradle her face, his thumb tracing the siyala there.

"It has made me wonder," she said softly, "how it will be to lie with a man who knows how to love me. Has made me want that, Apsimar." She reached up and placed a hand on his chest, thrilling at the slight tremor that went through him as she did so. "And yes, it has changed me." Taking his hand, she placed it over her heart, seeing him swallow hard as he cupped the high swell of her breast. "That rhythm you feel under your palm," she said. "That is my grief – and my power. For I have taken them, Apsimar, and I have made them one and the same."

He raised his eyes to hers, and she saw the naked longing in their depths, felt it shiver through her.

"My grief," she said in a low voice, "will be the power that drives the Arabs from the sands – and leads men where they would not go." She stepped forward, feeling him groan as her body came against the hard length of him. "I do not wish to be your wife," she murmured. "But I need the man you are, Apsimar. I need it."

His arms came around her, and his mouth took hers, hard and demanding and hotter than the desert wind.

10

ILLIBERIS

You, who are daughters of Aurariola, bear your father's name. When you marry you will take the name of your husband. It was not always thus. Not for the women of Illiberis, when I was young; not for the women of the Amazigh, ever. Men come and go. Women may take many of them in their lives. To name ourselves by a man is to brand ourselves with smoke.

The Lady of Aurariola, to her granddaughters
Al Andalus, AD 752

Dahiya met the horse keeper from Illiberis the next day as she stood on the docks to bid farewell to Apsimar.

"It will be a long voyage," he said, moving to kiss her, in full view of his men.

"It was a long night," she murmured, stepping back and drawing her tagelmust over her face.

His expression darkened. "Am I to be so quickly forgotten?"

"We are creatures of war, Apsimar." She felt the desert fall about her like a shield, seeing the moment when he felt it divide

64

them. "We will always leave to do what we must and enjoy each other when we may."

"It is not enough, Dahiya," he growled.

"It must be enough."

She turned to leave, and his hand closed about hers.

"You leave easily," he said harshly.

"Ah, but I am of the sands," she said, raising her face with pride. "In the desert, we learn early to live – and to die. We learn what it is to love – and to leave."

She stepped away from him. "When you sail," she said, "do not turn back. We will meet again. Look ahead to that day, not behind to a night that is already gone."

He spun from her in anger and stood at the prow of his dromon, legs planted strongly apart, arms folded. His crimson cloak streamed out behind him on the brisk morning wind, and his golden hair gleamed in the winter sun.

Dahiya forced her face to remain composed so that when she turned back, no man would know her feelings. She felt the hard heat of his body inside her still, her skin holding the memory of his flesh long after the sight of it had gone.

She must be a leader of men. There was no line of women who had gone before for her to follow, only the dim legend of Tin Hinan, a story told about the fire. Dahiya must forge her own path. If any man suspected she had given herself to the Greek commander, she knew that path would die before ever she began to walk it.

"He is a man to be proud of."

A woman almost as tall as Dahiya herself stood close by. She was a foreigner, clad in a fine woollen gown cut low at the breast, lined with rich embroidery. She wore her dark hair coiled high on her head and a silver serpent torque about her neck. It had eyes of brilliant sapphire, which flashed as they caught the sun. She had a determined face and eyes of a strange, deep gold, like those Dahiya had once seen on a desert cat.

"You are Dahiya of the Jerawa." The woman held out her arm. "I am Acantha, wife of Paulus, Count of Illiberis, in Spania."

Dahiya stared at the arm. She had never greeted a woman of

Spania. Hesitantly she reached out and clasped the arm at the elbow, following Acantha's example.

"Is this how the women of Spania name themselves?" Dahiya asked curiously. "As the wife of a man?"

"Do you not do so?" Acantha was equally curious.

"No. I am the daughter of Safiyya and Tabat. I will always be the daughter of Safiyya and Tabat, for this cannot be changed." Latin felt alien on Dahiya's tongue. The foreigners she knew spoke Greek. She used Latin but rarely, and she found the formation of the sentences awkward. "I may take many men during my life," she explained to Acantha. "Why would I name myself by something that is like to be fleeting?"

"And your children?" Acantha asked. "How will they name themselves?"

"They will know to whom they are born and will name their allegiance to their fathers. Such is our way." Dahiya covered her belly with one hand. "I think I will bear Apsimar's child," she said, as if to herself.

"You have been his lover for a long time, then," said Acantha.

"No. One night only. But I feel it." She saw the incomprehension on the other woman's face and thought that perhaps Spanish women did not feel water in their bodies or hear the whispers of their ancestors on the wind, as did women of the desert. Changing the subject, she said: "Ilyan tells me you bring horses of great quality."

Acantha inclined her head. "Illiberis is famed for horseflesh," she said.

"I have never met a woman of Spania, nor seen horses from there."

"We do not often travel alone. And I can take you now to view the horses."

"If you do not often travel alone," said Dahiya as they made their way to the yards below the palace, "why then are you here, selling horses?"

"In my family," said Acantha, "it is the women who know the secrets of horses. We are descended from the tribes of Illiberis, who worship the horse goddess still. I do not need my husband's permission to travel, and I did not ask it." Her face darkened. "He would not approve of my coming here," she said curtly, "nor of the reason I am come."

"It is not only to sell your horses," guessed Dahiya.

"No." Acantha's eyes flashed gold in the sun. "It is not."

They did not speak again of her reasons for coming, but instead they spent the day drilling the horses she had brought on the flat ground below the city, where the old circus had once hosted games of savagery.

"I have never seen horses of the like." Dahiya reined in a tall, black mount at the end of the ground, her eyes shining. "I need only think a command, and the horse obeys it. I can ride with no hand on the reins, and it turns at the slightest change in balance; I fire my arrows, and the horse leaps when I require it and seems to pause mid-air when I do not."

Acantha smiled as if Dahiya had praised her own child. "We raise them thus," she said simply. "I know the lineage and nature of every animal in our herd."

"It is a gift." Dahiya nodded. "I will ask Ilyan if he will purchase them all."

Acantha looked away for a moment, as if giving her next words consideration, then said carefully: "They say you know as much as Ilyan, and more, of the movements on your shores."

Dahiya turned down her mouth. "Not, perhaps, as much as Ilyan in some things," she said. "I would say that Ilyan and I have… different knowledge. Complementary knowledge."

"I would say," said Acantha without hesitation, "that it is your knowledge I need. If you are prepared to share it, I would make a gift of these horses – not to Ilyan, but to you."

Dahiya's eyebrows lifted. "For what purpose do you seek knowledge?"

Acantha met her eyes, her own a hard, burnished bronze. "For revenge," she said.

"Ah." Dahiya did not smile. "Revenge is something I understand well."

"Yes," said Acantha. "I thought it might be."

Dahiya looked at the other woman, taking in the hard, set mouth and the fire lurking deep behind her eyes.

"You have grief," she said quietly.

Acantha inclined her head stiffly. "I have lost all four of my children. My sons to war. And my daughter" – she swallowed hard – "my daughter, this summer past."

"And the revenge you seek?"

Acantha's lips thinned. "For wrongs done to my family," she said tightly. "Wrongs I cannot prove, but that I know." She thumped her chest. "Here," she said. "I know them here."

Dahiya nodded slowly. *Perhaps,* she thought, *Spanish women are not so different from us after all.*

Dismounting, she touched the brand emblazoned on the horse's shoulder. It was an intriguing symbol: a single line, embraced by entwined serpents.

"This symbol is not strange to me," she said. "I have seen it before, carved in the stone of forgotten temples, a memory of times and peoples past. Your line, I think, is an ancient one."

Acantha nodded assent. "There was a time," she said, "when my people and yours worshipped the same gods. Gods unknown to the Romans or the Greeks after them. Unknown to the Goths who rule my country now."

"But *you* know these gods?"

"I hear their whispers." Acantha met her eyes steadily. "They are remembered in our caves, where my ancestors live still, where the daughters of Illiberis are taken before they can speak."

A shadow of pain crossed her face, there and gone.

Dahiya thought of the deep, red ravine in the mountains she called home. The old women had taken her there for her siyala, so that she might sit amongst paintings drawn by hands older than memory and feel the power of those who had gone before her as the seeds of fertility were drawn on her own face. Like this, the women had told her, the sons born of those seeds would come to be imbued with the power of their ancestors and know who they were.

Acantha, she thought, *would understand that place.*

"We will ride into the desert together," said Dahiya, coming to a decision. "The air is clean, and things are known and seen that cannot be understood amidst stone and men. I will take you to the place of pictures, the place of my ancestors, and we will speak of this revenge you seek. Perhaps I can help you; perhaps not. Revenge is a matter for the wronged, and it cannot be taken on another's behalf. If it is right for you to take this vengeance, then we will know."

"I cannot ride for long," said Acantha. "I must return to Spania and to my husband." Her mouth twisted. "I have a grandchild," she said hoarsely. "The daughter of my daughter."

"Then we will ride as soon as we may."

Dahiya looked around at the tall city walls and shivered with distaste.

"I am glad to leave," she said. "I do not like these places of power and politics. In the sands, all people are equal."

They slept a night more in the palace, and when dawn broke, Dahiya rode from Septem at the head of a herd of Illiberis horses, and Acantha rode at her side.

11

GODS

In this new Spania, this place the Moors call Al Andalus, men pray to their God from books. Jew, Christian, Muslim — they make laws in the name of their books and argue over which is correct. But long before men and their books, there were laws of earth and water. Laws that women held and men obeyed. One day you will be women, and you, too, will know these laws, will feel them, even if you do not understand their meaning. This is the gift of being women — and the curse, also.

The Lady of Aurariola, to her granddaughters
Al Andalus, AD 752

They rode hard to the south and east, driving the herd before them. In the north, grazing was plentiful. Dahiya sent Zdan and Igider with scouts to the south, into the sands, to summon her father's allies. She and Acantha rode with a handful of Ilyan's men, who maintained a respectful — and slightly awed — distance. When they made camp, Acantha and Dahiya spoke in low murmurs away from the fire. Often they talked late into the night. Their discussion roamed over many subjects, and Dahiya discovered they had more in common than she could have imagined.

"The horse-herding tribes you speak of," she asked curiously one night. "It is they who lived on your land before Roman or Greek. Were they conquered, then?"

"My people," said Acantha, "once ruled a nation they called Tartessos. It was as great a nation – greater, perhaps – than that we know now as Spania. We were famed for our metal work" – she touched the serpent at her throat – "and traded throughout the Circle of Lands. Gods walked amongst us, and we knew their favour. We had our own written language and laws." She glanced at Dahiya. "I know this to be true," she said quietly. "I have seen it, in our caves. Our people speak of it, under the dreaming moon and when it is time for our stories to be told. It is from those times that my family know the secrets of horseflesh, the spirits of animals, and how to use them."

Dahiya nodded. "It is like this, too, for our people."

"You ask how we were conquered." Acantha clasped her arms about her knees and drew them in close. "Some say the waters came first, others that war angered the spirits of land and animal and brought water over us. Either way, our great cities sank beneath the tides. A time of famine came, and much of our wisdom was lost. Then came men and boats from across the seas. We rose again, warred again, fell again. The tribes retreated, further and further inland, to caves and mountains." She stared into the dark night. "Illiberis," she said quietly, "is one of the old places. My people have ruled it as far as memory goes. The Romans, when first they came, named the southern provinces 'Bætica' – and they named our family 'Bæticus', in acknowledgment of our ownership." She raised her chin proudly. "The women of Illiberis have married Roman, Greek, and Goth," she said, "but always, there has been a woman of the tribes on our land. It is the women who keep the rivers alive and know the secrets of our earth. The men who marry us know this, even if it is they who argue in the councils of our kings. Our land may have been conquered. It may be ruled by men who know nothing of it. But it will always be ours. It lives within us, and we within it."

Her hand covered her chest in a gesture so reminiscent of the Jerawa that Dahiya was taken aback.

"We, too, believe as you do," she said. "Our histories are truly alike." She glanced at Acantha. "Perhaps," she said thoughtfully, "the sea that divides us was once not so wide as it is now."

"Perhaps." Acantha met her eyes. "Where do you take me?" she asked bluntly. "The days pass, and the moon makes almost another turn. I cannot remain much longer distant from my family."

"I am taking you to the place of my own ancestors." Dahiya glanced up at the sky; the moon was waning, almost a thin crescent. "We will arrive when the moon is dark. You will see there what you must."

* * *

THE NIGHT before the new moon made the desert a strange place. Mountains loomed dark against the stars. Nothing moved on the rocky track as the two women climbed upward. Not even the call of a bird disturbed the silence.

It was a small death, the dark moon, a time when the earth slept and awaited the renewal of the mother's face.

Men forget this, Dahiya thought. *They forget that their wars and their victories mean nothing to the earth. They bow to her cycles every day, in the planting of their crops and the nights they choose to ride, the times they can make war and those of peace. The moon and sun and stars dance about the earth, guiding their every move, and yet none allow themselves to feel it.*

She felt peace in Acantha's company. The other woman seemed equally untroubled by the stillness and silence, unlike the men, none of whom would leave the camp on the dark moon. They feared the ghosts of the desert, the singing sands and the spirits who wandered them.

At the dark of the moon, men said, things wander the earth that have no right there.

Dahiya felt the presence in the air of those energies, long dormant, able to emerge now in the absence of the moon's bright gaze. She did not fear them; they were another part of earth. She walked through their soft tendrils, further into the mountains. She

72

was aware of Acantha's steady breathing at her side, and she knew her companion understood the night as she herself did.

The track abruptly rose, taking them amongst the tall cliffs until they stood at the mouth of a narrow defile. Dahiya paused and raised her hand to make the sign of protection, feeling a faint shiver when she saw Acantha make the same one.

It was strange, this understanding they shared. Dahiya was glad she had brought the other woman here.

They entered the defile and followed it down, into the rock, until the way narrowed into a long corridor between two sheer red cliffs. Dahiya reached into a rock hollow for the old silver box that held a tallow candle; she withdrew it and replaced it with the one she had brought. Lighting a small bundle of grass from the coal she had brought with her, she lit the candle.

The flame threw strange shadows onto the rock as she stepped into the pathway of paintings. The ground here was oddly warm, the rocks retaining heat after the day's sun, radiating it into the earth underfoot. It seemed to pulsate, a vital rhythm in the deep black.

She walked slowly, moving the candle to cast light onto vivid markings made by hands more ancient than any could remember. There were beasts and warriors, strange spirits, and battles long forgotten.

She allowed the voices to emerge from the rock, whispers from the past that sang to her as she trod the sand quietly: snatches of sound from time beyond time.

She emerged where an underground spring fed a shallow pool in the rock. She sat beside it on a stone worn smooth by those who had come before her, and Acantha sat opposite, on the ground. Dipping their fingertips into the pool, both women passed water over their faces. Dahiya tasted mineral droplets on her tongue. She planted the candle into the ground behind her, so it cast a soft, shadowed light. Closing her eyes, she began softly to hum, and, across the fire, Acantha's voice joined her own, melding and weaving through the still air.

At first it was a soft vibration, but then the rock began to feel it and pass the reverberations back and forth, until the walls themselves held the sound, and the humming passed from the women to the stone and into the earth and back, the water on the shallow pool shimmering with movement.

Dahiya felt the sound enter her body, opening her from the ground up, splitting away the form she wore and entering deep into a place far beyond her skin and bone. She felt it take her and breathed deeply, surrendering to the sound.

She was not aware of when she ceased humming and the images began. The vibration was travelling through her, and with it came pictures, tumbling through her mind in an elusive combination of knowing and suggestion:

Two horses, white and black, lying in a pool of blood, their manes becoming two serpents, twined about a stick.

A head etched into silver, the head becoming a helmet, standing before the walls of Carthage.

A terrible battle, iron and blood, triumph and despair.

Golden eyes behind a bow. Loneliness. Terrible thirst, pain, alone in the sands – excruciating pain! She wanted to scream with the ripping pain and terrible fear. Loneliness, despair… and again, swords and blood…

A cord made of the serpents, tenuous but strong – the cord must not break.

And again, the walls.

Carthage.

Falling. Falling in stone and screams and Arabic.

"When Carthage falls, so will Altava."

Dahiya's eyes sprang open.

Her heart was pounding. She looked about wildly, reaching for the candle and holding it high, searching for the voice. But there was only Acantha, staring at her with the same wide-eyed shock. Dahiya knew it was not the other woman who had spoken.

There was nobody there; she had known it, truly, yet the voice had seemed more real than anything she had witnessed there before.

Dahiya had sat in the pathway of paintings many times. Its cryptic visions were no stranger to her – but never had a voice spoken aloud with such clarity.

The humming had ceased. Only uneasy ripples on the pool bore evidence of their existence. Somewhere beneath the earth the sound still reverberated, causing the water to lap gently at the sides of the rock.

Dahiya dipped her fingers in again and felt a slight shock as she dripped water onto her face. It was alive, silvery to the touch, causing her to shiver despite the warmth of the rock.

The women sat in silence for a long moment, and Dahiya sensed that Acantha, too, was trying to make sense of what she had seen, knowing that by the time they left the caves, only the barest impressions would remain.

She dripped candlewax onto a flat stone and used the sharp edge of another to make marks that would remind her, when time had passed, of what seemed important.

"The cord must not break." It was Acantha who spoke, her voice husky and coarse from disuse.

"You, also, saw this?"

Acantha nodded. Leaning forward, she drew the pattern Dahiya had seen, a more complex depiction of that on the horses from Illiberis, like two snakes entwined.

Dahiya took the stone from her and drew a circle, with the barest profile inside.

"A head etched in silver," she said.

Acantha nodded. She shuddered, then, and Dahiya knew the other woman had felt the same agony she had.

Pain in the sands.

She drew big dunes.

"When Carthage falls," she said slowly, "so will Altava."

The blood drained from Acantha's face. "I heard," she whispered, "that when Carthage falls – so will Spania."

The women stared at each other across the shimmering water, the flame flickering wildly in the still air.

"Is it possible," said Dahiya harshly, "that both are true?"

The older woman looked at her, and Dahiya felt Acantha's strength, the wisdom of those who have borne children and lost them, the cycle of a woman.

"Time will twist our recollections," Acantha said, "shaping them this way and that, to become something to suit a selfish purpose. Make a mark that will keep their meaning clear to you, a reminder

to accept what you heard and saw, and simply live it as it comes."
Raising her knife, she made a cut in her own leg, high above the
knee. Two thin lines of blood appeared, a third making a cross
section between them.

"The break in the walls," she said. "And the cord that must not
break." She looked at Dahiya. "The cord, I think, is tied to my
land."

"And the walls," said Dahiya, "to mine."

"And yet they are joined."

"Yes," said Dahiya. "They are."

Do not bring this forward with my seeing it, she thought fiercely, even
though she knew the seeing of it could not make it happen out of its
proper time. *Let me make my people safe. Let me try to change it. I must try.*

And she felt the sudden weight of her ability to see, the horrible
curse of knowing the futility of all they fought for – but knowing she
must yet try.

"The end is not the way," Acantha said quietly, as if she heard
her thoughts. "We see what will be. We know nothing of how it
comes or why it is important. We see the future, but we may walk
only in the present. It is for us to know the magic we live each day –
and to feel it, with every footstep."

Her voice quieted Dahiya's soul, and they sat for a long time in
stillness, allowing the warm reassurance of the ages to soothe them.

"Your revenge," said Dahiya finally.

Acantha shook her head. The water had stilled, and the candle
burned close to the earth. "The revenge is not to be mine," she said.
"It belongs to another of my line." A shadow crossed her face. "I
am the way by which these things are wrought," she said quietly,
"but I am not their carrier. I will not live the events that I saw here
today."

She met Dahiya's eyes. "But you," she said, with certainty, "you
will live it all. One day, perhaps, you will know those who bear these
symbols, and it may fall to them to take my revenge. If you are willing, I will give you my tale. Like this, I might leave it here and return
to my home with my heart clean of darkness."

The women spoke deep into the night, and Dahiya heard Acantha's story of pain and betrayal, of blood and death. She heard it as

the new moon grew on the underside of the earth, as the soft dawn lit the cliffs ochre and rose.

In the morning, they parted ways. Acantha rode for the coast in the company of two of Ilyan's men. Dahiya watched her go, the tall, straight back disappearing into the horizon, and she felt a strange loss she had never known for her own mother. In the time they had ridden together, Acantha had seemed more than mother or friend. She had seemed a companion of Dahiya's soul.

Dahiya touched the raw scar on her leg, which matched Acantha's own. She felt the power of the woman within her, and the grief of her tale, mingle with Dahiya's own, becoming part of the strength she would need to face the life to which she had been born.

Dahiya of the Jerawa turned her face east to meet the rising sun.

"Come," she said to the men she led. "Now we ride for Thamugadi – and to war."

12

ILLUSION

Thamugadi, modern day Timgad, Algeria

I have lived long enough to know that all rule is illusion.

The Lady of Aurariola, to her granddaughters
Al Andalus, AD 752

The old city of Thamugadi had once been a rich place of scholars and merchants. Dahiya stood in a deserted courtyard where sand gathered on the cracked tiles. An old fountain stood dry in the centre. Behind her soared the high, vaulted ceiling of a room built to hold books. Once, she knew, men had gathered here to study and ponder questions of philosophy amidst a thriving city. Now the shelves stood empty, and men gathered in the shadow of crumbling walls to ponder the question of who would lead them to battle.

"How many?" she asked, without turning.

"Two thousand. Perhaps a few more." Zdan came to stand

behind her. "They wonder where you are, Dahiya. What they are here for."

"They will find out soon enough." Dahiya turned away from the scene below. "Did the boy I sent to our adwwar return?"

Zdan nodded and gestured behind him. "He returned not an hour ago." He looked curiously at her. "An odd mission you sent him upon, was it not?"

Dahiya did not answer. Instead, she beckoned the young boy into the courtyard, murmuring greetings as he approached.

"You got what I sent you for," she said, eyeing the heavy object the boy carried in a sack.

He nodded. "It was not difficult," he said. "The Ifren did not know its value, and they did not notice me entering the adwwar. I found it lying forgotten in a corner of your father's house." Realising his mistake, he coloured and began to stammer apologies, which Dahiya waved off impatiently.

"Tabat is dead," she said bluntly. "But I am not. And so long as I carry his sword and wear this" – she picked up the sack – "men will know the amgar of the Jerawa rides still."

"Dahiya." It was Igider who spoke, from the corner of the court-yard. He was tired and covered in dust. "Apsimar is here," he said, coming toward her. "I have told him to wait where you ordered." His mouth twisted. "He did not like taking orders from me," he said.

"No." Dahiya smiled inwardly. "Apsimar is not a man accustomed to taking orders."

The boy's eyes had widened at the mention of Apsimar's name. "The Greek commander is here?" he said breathlessly. He looked at her with something akin to awe. "And he takes orders from you?"

Dahiya gave him her most imperious stare, quelling the tremor within. "You may return to your camp," she said. "Please spread the word that I will address the clan leaders in the camp, at sunset."

"You do realise," said Igider dryly, watching the boy go, "that by sunset, all the men of the clans will know Apsimar is here – and that you ordered him?"

Dahiya's eyes gleamed in the late afternoon sun. "I am counting upon it," she said softly.

* * *

As the sun blazed the last hours of daylight, Dahiya stood alone in the deserted courtyard.

She reached into the sack and touched the curved horns of the war helmet.

Everything depended on this moment. If the Jerawa did not accept her as amgar, Apsimar's support would mean nothing. No logic would convince them, nor argument at a council. She must take them now, in this moment, or forever accept that the role of amgar could not be hers. There could be no second chance.

Once, in centuries beyond memory, men of her tribe had worn the helmet of Ghurzla into battle. The metal had been beaten into the shape of a bull's head. The horns, it was said, were once real and had been blessed by the bull god himself when he walked the earth. The helmet was made of iron, and the horns rose above it in a great arc. Once drawn over the head, the helmet hid the face completely, so the wearer became the fearsome bull god, Ghurzla, himself.

For many years now, the helmet had been worn only in ceremony: during the anointing of a new amgar or on the solemn night before battle. It was too heavy, Tabat had told his daughter, for any man of their age to wear into battle.

"For it was wrought," he had told her, "in a time when gods walked the earth amongst us and men fought astride horses the like of which have not been seen in many years. Those days are gone, and the men who rode those horses are gone with them. Now Ghurzla watches over us. He sends us to battle. But he does not ride amongst us, for we have yet to find a leader worthy of his strength."

Dahiya drew a deep breath and raised the helmet before her.

She stared at the dying sun and thought of the vision she had seen, of the walls of Carthage falling beneath the Arabic sword.

If Carthage falls, so does Altava.

The eyes of the bull were dark holes in the helmet. To Dahiya they seemed to be waiting rather than empty, a space destined to be filled.

Feeling a surge of excitement and dread leap through her, she thought: *We no longer have time, my father, to wait for your leader of strength. Now is the time for those who would lead to stand forward and do so.*

She touched Ahar at her side and turned to the crumbling archway. Beyond it, Igider and Zdan waited with one of Apsimar's men.

Dahiya took a deep breath and strode through.

She stood before the two men of her kel. Their eyes widened as they saw the helmet in her hands.

Zdan led forward the great black warhorse that had become her favourite during the time she rode with Acantha. It stood a full forearm above any animal belonging to the Jerawa, gleaming like polished ebony in the last rays of the sun. She nodded at Apsimar's man.

"Go to him," she said. "You know my instructions."

The man looked up at the tall woman on the powerful animal, taking in the great helmet poised before her, the hair in a rippling sea down her back, and the ruby between her eyes. He nodded once and ran to do her bidding.

Dahiya looked at Zdan and Igider.

"Come," she said. "It is time."

Dahiya led the two men from the old city down the remains of a wide stone road. The dying red ball lit them from behind so they were silhouetted in the dusk and hard to distinguish. Following them, in a long, silent stream, walked the horses of Illiberis, as if led by an invisible thread.

Men emerged from their tents, drawn by the theatre of the moment and the oddity of the sight. As Dahiya reached the first of them, chattering lowered to a murmur, then, when they realised she held the helmet of Ghurzla, to a shocked silence.

She had both hands on the helmet, and when she drew to a halt, she did so with no more than a subtle shift of her form, so it seemed as if the warhorse were part of her, standing proudly to attention, staring at the crowd with the same disdain as his mistress. The ruby glowed with its own inner fire, daring any man to speak.

Dahiya waited until she could discern, in the faces before her, those men who had sat at her father's fire as leaders.

Then she held the helmet high over her head. The dying sun was a fiery ball hanging directly between the two bull horns, as if placed there by a divine hand. A ripple of superstitious awe went through the watching men.

Dahiya lowered the helmet, very slowly, over her head.

She felt the wave of power when the iron settled about her – a power older than the iron in which it resided, older than the horns above it. Power made by the men and women who had worn it before her, by the blood they had shed and the agony they had known. Power that belonged to Amazigh and Altava and which lived in the blood of Tabat's daughter as it had in her father, and as the great war mask settled upon Dahiya's shoulders, she knew she had been born to wear it.

She pulled the gleaming length of Ahar from its scabbard, and as she did, the men before her drew back in alarm, for behind her, from around the walls of Thamugadi, rode a Greek horde, led by a blazing blond commander in a blood-red tunic.

"Men of the desert!"

Fire leaped through Dahiya's veins, and the black horse plunged and surged beneath her. Dahiya wheeled it and thrust her arm into the air.

"*Jerawa!*" she screamed, and her cry unleashed the voices of the men before her, men who had followed Ghurzla in their dreams and fought for Altava from their swaddling.

"*Jerawa!*" they roared as one, the sound of drawn steel echoing from the cliffs about them.

"See those whom Ghurzla commands!" She spun her horse with only her legs, her upraised arm encompassing the army on the hill and the herd of horseflesh standing in a proud, still line behind her. "See the power he grants us!"

She made the gesture Acantha had taught her and, as one, every horse came to its knees, heads bowed before her.

The warlike cry turned to a collective sigh of wonder, and the men stared at the god who faced them with the head of the bull and a sword lit by red fire.

"My father's adwwar was attacked in the night," she cried, her voice clear and strong across the plain, "by men who thought to make Tabat's daughter their slave. To make Ghurzla their servant. To make the Jerawa no more than a memory!"

"*Tabat!*" They roared her father's name, but she heard the uncertainty in their voice and knew the moment was close. Holding the horse completely still with her body, not a muscle moving, she dropped her voice so men must strain to hear her.

"The man who sought to defile me is dead." The words echoed off the iron helmet, bouncing across the sea of faces in an eerie sound that made men draw back, murmuring amongst themselves. "He died with the taste of my body in his mouth and my father's blood in the place where his spirit would leave. He died with Ghurzla's force choking the breath from his body."

They were silent now, watching her.

"The men of the Ifren hold my adwwar still," she said, her voice dropping even lower, becoming deathly cold. "But we will not kill them, for such men do not deserve the taste of my father's sword."

There was a rumbling at this, a swell, and she knew the time for theatre had come.

"It is Ghurzla who claims their lives!" She thrust her head back and threw the words into the gloaming, feeling the energy gather in the crowd around her. "Ghurzla – and Altava!"

"*Altava!*" they roared.

"In Kairouan," she cried, her voice clear and strong across the plain, "the caliph's army awaits us. Men who believe this land is theirs. Men who believe their God is greater than those of the Amazigh. Men who believe we are little more than grains of the desert itself, to be trodden underfoot. Are we such creatures?"

"*No!*" they roared, howling with fury at her words.

"And yet we are!" She whirled to face them once again. "We are the sand, and we are the sun! We are the whispers that torture in the night and the winds that blind in the day. We are the heat that closes the throat and the mirage men see when they long for water. All of this we are, if only we will fight together as one people!"

Her horse spun and plunged, so tightly it seemed she would be thrown into the dust, and men sighed as she surged up once more, awestruck at the snarling black horse and the god who commanded it.

"Will you fight?" She hurled the challenge at them, holding Ahar high over her head. "Will you follow Ghurzla and Ahar, and the blood of Tabat? Will you join the army of legions and drive the Arab dogs from our shores forever? Will you fight for Ghurzla – and Altava?"

"*Ghurzla!*" they roared back as one man, surging forward to surround her, to touch the divinity that rode amongst them. "*Altava!*"

"Give me your swords!" she cried, spinning the horse once again.

Then there was nothing but the clatter of steel as men laid down their blades before her and bent their heads to Ghurzla, to the bull god of war, for all knew that none who was not worthy could wear his likeness, nor carry the Lion, Ahar.

"*Dahiya!*" cried Igider, the cry coming from behind his cupped hand, so none knew from whence it began. On the distant ridge, the Greeks echoed the cry into the purple gloaming: "*Dahiya!*"

And as the mountains rang with the sound of men screaming her name, beneath the great iron helmet, Dahiya, Queen of the Jerawa, felt the blood of her ancestors thrill through her and the power of her grief grow triumphant within her.

I am ready, she thought exultantly.

On the distant ridge, Apsimar sat on his horse, still and unmoved amidst the Amazigh clamour. She stared at him, waiting, but he did not raise his spear in silent acknowledgement, nor make any indication that he had seen her triumph.

She watched him until, finally, the tall figure turned his horse and rode from sight.

13

VENGEANCE

Arabs hold their vengeance like sustenance, feeding upon it until it becomes an appetite of its own. Goths seek retribution as honour and call it justice. But Amazigh, who are born to shifting sands, know that revenge is an empty chalice. They understand that balance comes to all who live, designed by forces beyond our control and wrought by unseen hands. Though revenge may belong to the wronged, a true leader knows that no wrong can be truly righted unless the sands deem it so.

The Lady of Aurariola, to her granddaughters
Al Andalus, AD 752

Dahiya rode into her father's adwwar carrying the helmet of Ghurzla before her, with a hundred mounted men silent and menacing behind her.

"The Ifren are gone."

It was one of the old women who stepped forward. She had known Dahiya from infancy, and she looked at her now with curiosity.

"A man came from the Ifren adwwar," she said. "He ordered

85

those of his kel to depart, leaving a small guard here, for our safety only. They, too, rode from here not two days ago, when news came of your approach."

Zdan moved forward. "My father?" he asked roughly.

The old woman shook her head. "What men were here died the night the Ifren came," she said.

Zdan looked over her shoulder, and an expression of relief flooded his face as two slender figures ran forward, throwing themselves into his arms.

"We thought you dead," cried his sisters, raining their kisses upon his face.

"Our mother?" He held them at arm's length, studying their faces.

When they shook their heads slowly, he wept, holding them close.

"She died protecting us," said the younger of his sisters. "She sent us to the mountain caves to hide when first we heard them come."

"She took four of them before she died," said the elder. "We are proud of her, Zdan."

"But you — you were not harmed?"

"No." The elder sister stood back and gazed at Dahiya, something like awe in her eyes. "But even if we were," she said, "what matter, when we have an amgar who will take such revenge for our people?"

A murmur rose amongst the women and children of the Jerawa.

"We know how Yedder died." It was the old woman who spoke again. She gestured at the Jerawa around her. "They told us, the women who rode here from the Ifren. The men looked away in shame, but the women told us what you did." She stared at Dahiya in fascination. "Not since Tin Hinan has a woman led us. But now you do, Dahiya, daughter of Tabat."

"We want what you took." It was Zdan's younger sister who stepped forward, her eyes flashing. "Revenge for the wrongs done to us. Justice for our amgar and retribution to the Ifren for daring to take what does not belong to them. I will ride beside you, Dahiya of the Jerawa, and I will fight, as my brother does, as my mother did. I will fight – and die if I must."

The women around her threw back their heads and ululated into the desert air, screaming their rage at what had been done them.

Dahiya listened, still and quiet on her horse.

When the sound faded out, she said one word: "No."

They looked at her, hurt and indignation warring on their faces.

"But you fight," said Zdan's sister angrily. "You are amgar now. You of all people understand that we, too, can fight."

"I do not doubt for a moment that you can fight with the passion of every man here." Dahiya met her eyes steadily. "And I will need you to do so, sooner than you might think. I will need every sword you have, in the wars to come."

"But you will not help us take revenge upon the Ifren?"

The woman who asked the question bore the marks of savage attack on her face. Dahiya winced to think of what scars she bore inside and beneath the ragged cloth that covered her.

"You would let this wrong stand against the Jerawa," whispered the woman, spitting on the ground in fury. "My husband would have slaughtered the man who took me. He would not have rested until he had seen justice for what was done to me. Is this what we are to expect of our amgar? That she will stand by whilst the women and children of her kel are reaved in the open and advise us to do nothing but run to the mountains? Will all men know they may ride upon us with impunity? What honour is this? What kind of amgar is this?"

Angry murmurs rose behind her, and women clutched their children close.

Dahiya did not move. She covered her chest again, looking around at the gathered crowd.

"I do not expect your allegiance," she said quietly. "Your choices must be your own. I know only what I must do. If it is revenge you seek, I will not command you otherwise. Revenge belongs to every heart. Only you can decide if you must have it. I took my own and judge no person for doing the same. But I cannot help you take your revenge. If I do, I risk all we are."

"Why do you say this?" It was Zdan's sister who spoke. "What else can be more important than ensuring our enemies are defeated?"

Dahiya met her eyes steadily. "Nothing," she said, "is more important than that. But your question assumes the Ifren are the greatest enemy we face – and that is not true."

Dahiya looked around at the expectant faces. "An Arabic army awaits in Kairouan. If we waste time fighting amongst ourselves, we cannot hope to defeat it."

"I could leave men here to guard you." She met their eyes. "I could ride upon the Ifren." She gestured behind her. "I have enough with me to slaughter every man of their kel in revenge for what was done here to you. And yet after they die, still I must ride to Kairouan to face the Arabs."

They muttered at that. Dahiya held up a hand.

"We are people of the desert," she said. "The sands are our home. Our mother." She brought her clenched fist over her chest. "The desert will hold us, and keep us, that we may fight again – and again. We will never allow the Arabs to take our mother. But to defend her, we must first live."

"And what is it to live," said the woman in tattered cloth, bitterly, "if it is without pride – without honour?"

"Because every man slaughtered in the taking of revenge against the Ifren is one less sword against an army that already outnumbers us ten to one." There was no gentleness in Dahiya's voice now, nor mercy in the eyes that flashed amber at the woman. "Every man dead for your honour is one less the Arabs must cut down to take you for their own. And they *will* take you. They will take every man, woman, and child in their path, for to the men of the caliph, we are no more than animals. Is this the revenge you wish for?"

She stared at her accuser in the long silence that followed. It was the woman who dropped her eyes first.

Dahiya's horse plunged beneath her. "I had a choice!" She wheeled the animal with one hand to meet the watching faces. "This sword – this helmet – I could have turned from them. I could have bowed my head and given my body and my blessing to a man of our kel, asking him to carry them both for me, to fight in my name and for my blood. But I did not."

She stared out at them, allowing the grief and power to surge through her, allowing it to be her voice so her people might know her for what she was.

"I do not bear them because I want the power they bestow or because my father bore them before me. I bear them because they are mine, by blood and by pain, and because in them I carry your blood, your pain, also. I bear them because they are my burden to carry, just as you are my people to guard."

Her voice had risen as she spoke, and now tension hung in the air, her horse plunging and surging beneath her, the air crackling like the greatest of storms gathering overhead.

"When I leave here" – her voice echoed from the rock – "I will ride to the Ifren. I will command them to ride at my back. I will send them into battle first, ahead of my force, that they may have the chance to prove themselves men of honour once again – or die the cowards they were here, for the wrongs they did you."

Now they roared, a great guttural swell of anger and pain that thrilled the air.

"I will command the Ifren thus, and they will follow me or they will die. This, I can do for you. This alone. If it is not enough, then you must choose your own path, for this is the way I have chosen, and it is what I will do. I fight for the Jerawa – and I fight for my father's dream and the history of our people. I fight for Altava!"

"*Altava!*" they roared, and now they came forward, crowding her horse and calling her name.

Zdan's sister came forward, pressing her forehead to Dahiya's hand. "Amgar," she whispered, her eyes shining. "Amgar. One day I, also, will fight for you."

Dahiya gripped the girl's chin, feeling the heat of her power flow into the slender figure.

"Yes," she said fiercely, "and Altava will welcome your sword, as will I."

"*Altava!*" the girl shrieked, head back, howling her defiance to the desert sands.

One by one they came, crying and proud, screaming their alle-

giance and touching their leader, until finally there was only the
scarred and bitter woman left facing her.

"I will call you amgar," she said coldly. "But until a Jerawa
sword has found Ifren flesh, I do not forgive you, Dahiya, daughter
of Tabat."

"That is your right." Dahiya bowed before her, and the woman
gripped her arm, her eyes dark with pain and anger.

"The man who took me was named Badis. He wears my scar on
his face, across his left eye. When he lies suffering on the ground,
screaming for his mother, his guts on your sword – then I follow you.
Until then, it is just words."

Dahiya nodded.

"I understand," she said simply. She looked at the people of her
adwwar, meeting every eye, and gripped the woman's arm one last
time. Then she turned to the men behind her. "The Greeks are a
day ahead of us," she said. "We must ride."

14

WITCH

A woman who leads men fights her greatest battles before ever she takes the field. No skill with sword nor bravery in the face of death will win men to her cause. No strategy nor reason will convince them. Whilst a man builds his reputation with every victory, a woman will be judged anew with every conflict. Should she fail, men will say it is because she is a woman; should she win, men will look for the man they believe won for her. And should they find one, then they have their answer: she is a witch, who spellbound men to her cause.

Better a woman be thought witch from the beginning — and have men fear her as such.

The Lady of Aurariola, to her granddaughters
Al Andalus, AD 752

Dahiya maintained her camp away from Apsimar and the Greek forces.

She told herself it was because she was amgar of all the Jerawa now. She was a leader — a queen. Every day brought questions about alliances and strategy, petty squabbles amongst the thousands who followed her toward Aksil's camp near Kairouan.

91

But when evening fell and she saw, in the distance, the tall, bronzed figure standing in his customary posture with legs firmly planted wide apart, hands on hips, bellowing orders, snatches of which carried on the still desert gloaming, she knew herself for a liar.

Dahiya did not approach Apsimar's camp because she wanted him. She wanted him so much she felt the weakness in her belly like a sickness, her need for him pounding between her legs so she could barely sleep. She wanted him so badly she was afraid to so much as glance in his direction whilst her men were close, for men sought weakness in any leader – but they sought it doubly so in a young girl who had yet to prove herself in battle.

Dahiya knew she could allow no crack to show in the remote facade she presented. She had gained the advantage of shock and of mystery. Men were unsure of her in a way they would never be of a man. She was a woman who had dared to seize power, not by sitting in council and arguing her case, or by marrying a man she could control, but by claiming it as her right and refusing to countenance any opposition.

She knew that opposition existed still. She saw it in the smirks men cast her way when they thought she did not see, in the snide comments they made about battle that reminded her that they had wielded steel on the field and she had not. And as they came closer to Aksil's camp, the tension in her and those around her increased, for they all knew her claims to power would mean nothing if Aksil decided against them.

For all of those reasons, Dahiya knew she could not reach out to Apsimar. Her authority in part rested upon men's belief that the Greek commander bowed to her. If the Jerawa thought for a moment that it was she who bowed to Apsimar, they would turn upon her with a savagery that would make Yedder's attack seem paltry. The Jerawa bowed to no foreigner, Greek or otherwise. If they thought her Apsimar's whore, every advantage she had wrought was lost forever.

Apsimar, she knew, understood this. He led men. He knew the fragility of power, the shifting sands upon which authority was built.

And yet she felt his eyes upon her.

Sometimes it came in the morning, when they broke camp and Dahiya rode out ahead of the long line of men and horses. In the dim light of the predawn, she would first become aware of the smudge in the distance that signified the Greek lines. Then, as if drawn by an invisible thread, her eyes would invariably find him, customarily atop a crest, mounted as he watched his men pass. Even when his figure was no more than the suggestion of a silhouette, Dahiya could feel the searing heat of his eyes on her skin, and she knew he watched her as she did him. She felt his desire reach out to her own, his heat firing her own core until she could barely breathe for needing him.

But it was these times she found the hardest, Dahiya thought, not daring to look at where she knew he stood. Now, as the sun dropped behind the mountains and men took to their blankets. Now, when the desert fell silent and there were only the high stars and thoughts of love to keep her warm. Now, when she longed to turn to him and take solace from the solitary burden of leading just for a moment, to lose herself in his mouth and his hands and the driving force of him thrusting inside her.

Dahiya was barely aware she had sighed aloud until a slow chuckle came from behind her.

She froze.

"You should not be here," she muttered, even as she felt her resolve weaken, her body begin to betray her.

"If I am forced to endure one more night without you," Apsimar growled from behind the rocks, "it is not the Arabs my men will need to fear."

She felt him come close enough that his breath was warm on her neck. She forced herself to maintain her composure, staring out at the camp below as if she sat in contemplation, as she did every night at this time.

"And if men see us together" – she turned her face slightly to the side and down, so she felt rather than saw his lean figure behind her – "they will say it is your hand on Ahar, your mind guiding my reason."

"Would that be so terrible?" He stepped into focus, though still out of sight of the men below. He was frowning. "In Septem you spoke of ideas, a general plan. One I supported then and still do. But I begin to realise" – he reached out and grasped her chin, forcing her to face him – "that you plan to be amongst this force of Riders. That you intend to take the field with sword in hand and fight beside them."

"I am amgar." She met his eyes, her voice low. "It is what I must do."

"No, Dahiya." His voice was curt. "You might inspire men, unite them with your theatre. But you cannot fight amongst them."

She reared back from him. "You knew what I planned."

"No." He shook his head in a hard gesture. "I did not. And had you made it clear, I would not have so readily accompanied you." His hand turned her face to his, not gently. "I want you, Dahiya," he said roughly. "I want you so much I can barely breathe. But I am a commander of men first and your lover a distant second. You are untried in battle. Unproven. And do not speak of your father's raids, of the attack in the gorge – I have heard these tales of your legend, and I do not doubt your bravery with bow or steel. But Dahiya" – his finger gentled on her face, stroking the rigid line of her jaw – "war is not pretty speeches and an iron mask. It is not a night-time raid or a brief skirmish. It is strategy and forethought, steadiness and measure. Tight planning and rigid control. It takes experience, and it takes the respect of your entire force, a respect not easily won for any man, let alone –"

"Let alone a woman?" She stood abruptly and pushed him back, out of sight of the camp below and into the shadow of red rock, her eyes blazing and voice shaking. "Do you think I don't know my men follow your spear rather than my sword?" The bitterness in her tone took him back a step. "Why do you think I rode to Septem in beggar's robes and sought your support? I was clear, was I not, that men would not fight beside me, untried as I am. Did you think me deluded?"

"Then why try to do so now?" His voice was harsh. "Why not let them fight with me or Aksil?"

"If I were a man, would you doubt me?" Her voice was like a whiplash.

"Yes, Dahiya, I would!" He struck the rock by her head hard enough to crumble the stone there.

She moved closer to him, so their breath mingled. "You would doubt me," she said softly. "But you would give me the chance. You would allow me to try." She stepped closer still. "And you know it, Apsimar."

He was tense and still, his hand clenched on the rock the only sign of his tension.

"I fight because you stand behind me," she said, and though there was no denying the fury behind her eyes, her voice was steady enough. "Just as every man in the history of war must begin. I might fail, it is true. And if I do fail, I will never be permitted another attempt, for I am a woman, and men feel it beyond the natural order to fight beside my sword. But I have won the right to try, Apsimar. And whilst you may doubt me, just as every man who rides beside me yet does, you will not stop me. I will not allow it." She reached up, grasping his face fiercely. "I want you," she whispered. "I need you. But I will not allow want and need to rule my choices. It is I who lead the Jerawa. I will follow you. I will learn from you. But I will not cede to you, Apsimar, nor to any who would seek to rule me – or my people."

They stood a whisper apart, breath hard and hot between them, and she saw the moment her words broke the dam inside him and felt her own defences crumble with it.

"I have never known anything as beautiful – as wild – as you," he said roughly. "I think of you with sword in hand and I can't – Daya, I can't bear to think of it –"

"Then do not." Her voice, thick with desire, sounded strange to her, and when she touched his lips and he captured her fingers with them, she felt the touch at the very core of her. "Do not think of it," she said, gripping his face with both hands.

And despite everything she had told herself, despite every last grain of sense that told her this was dangerous, Dahiya backed away into the folds of rock still warm from the sun, turning to find Apsimar hard and hungry, and could do nothing but moan softly as his mouth found her.

"Do you know how it is," he murmured against her lips, "to see you every day and not be able to so much as touch you?"

His hands pulled her hard against him, sliding under the thin fabric of her robes to the swell of her buttocks, hitching her against the rock so he could move between her legs and press against the centre of her.

"Do you know how I have ached for this?" His hand slid around her thigh, and Dahiya gasped as his fingers began to stroke her, his mouth hot and demanding on her own. "Do you know how I have lain awake watching the stars turn, able to think of nothing but you – but this?" His clever fingers found her wet and ready for him, and Dahiya almost cried out when they slid inside her.

"Daya – *Iesu Xristu*, how I want you." His voice was hoarse, the piercing blue eyes cobalt with desire, and when his hands pushed her tunic up and his mouth found her breast, Dahiya could do nothing but press against him, asking with her body what she could not speak aloud.

He teased her with his tongue until she was squirming with need, her hands tangled in his hair. He pulled back and looked down at the tawny skin, the swollen tip of her damp from his mouth, and stared at her in wonder, one hand cradling her face.

"Just take me, Apsimar – now, hard, so I can carry you with me into battle, so I can feel you inside me…"

He groaned aloud at that and the last vestiges of his control broke, so he pushed down and plunged inside her, the iron-hard thickness of him filling her so completely that there was nothing but the deep, sensual rhythm of his body within her own, his hands holding her up against the rock as he surged inside her.

Dahiya felt the gloaming drop away and the sands come at her like a desert storm, then the fury consumed her, and she heard the sound of him roar his own release.

They sank, trembling, against the warm rock, lost in the bliss of their entwined limbs, still rocking together. Neither noticed the shadow that flitted silently through the thin trees and beyond, running in pale moonlight in the direction of Aksil's camp.

15

WHORE

Men believe there is no worse name for a woman than whore. But it is they who are enslaved by what lies between a woman's legs, they who will pay to take it, even embark upon war itself from desire. Whore is what men call the witch who does not fear their temporary possession of her body. You are shocked. I see it in your faces. But, my children, if you would seek power, then understand this: the woman who knows herself turns the word "whore" into a weapon so powerful no man can stand before it.

The Lady of Aurariola, to her granddaughters
Al Andalus, AD 752

"You are welcome, Dahiya."

There was a knowing tilt to Aksil's mouth that tainted his greeting and warned Dahiya to be on her guard.

"When you said you rode for Ilyan, and Septem, I had not realised you rode also for an army."

"Ghurzla finds his weapons where he may." Dahiya met his eyes steadily. They were less than a day's ride from the bulk of the Arabic army, so close she could feel her enemy's presence in the earth and see evidence of their grazing on the barren landscape. The thought of their animals grazing on the precious shrubs made her mouth tighten.

The Arabs did not belong here.

When Carthage falls, so will Altava.

She heard the words echo inside her and felt her resolve stiffen. Dahiya knew why she rode − and why she fought. She must never allow herself to forget.

Aksil's eyes dropped to the helmet of Ghurzla, which rested on the earth in front of Dahiya, her hands clasped between the fearsome horns in a calm attitude of possession.

"It would appear," Aksil said lightly, "that you claim close kinship to Ghurzla in these times, Dahiya, daughter of Tabat. No warrior has dared wear the helmet in living memory." He placed faint emphasis on the word "warrior": not enough − quite − to insult, but more than enough to make clear his implication that he did not consider Dahiya worthy of the name.

"In living memory, we have never faced the threat we do now. Such times create the warrior, Aksil."

He gave her a faintly derisory smile.

"But you are not a warrior, Dahiya," he said bluntly. "You have never swung that sword you carry, nor any other, in formal battle. Night raids and skirmishes in the sands are child's play. You know nothing of the way war is fought. I do not question your right to take council with the men; all here know your father allowed − even encouraged − you to speak. As his daughter, I honour your voice. But it is time for this theatre to cease, Dahiya. You cannot lead the men you bring here onto the field against a trained army led by an experienced commander. You will kill them and lose the day to the Arabs. I cannot believe that is what you want."

"It would appear those men do not share your opinion." Dahiya tilted her chin beyond the tent to the waiting horde. "Nor does Ilyan − nor Apsimar."

"Ah." The knowing smile was back, and Dahiya felt a momentary tremor as Aksil gazed out of the tent, his eyes resting on Apsimar's wide-legged figure in the distance. The Greek commander had given the Amazigh leaders time to meet before joining them; he knew, as well as Dahiya, the kind of opposition she would face.

"And how is it that you managed to so easily bend Ilyan, and Apsimar, to your will, Dahiya?" Aksil spoke without looking at her, but the low, insinuating tone said all she needed to know of his own thoughts. "How do they feel, I wonder," he mused, "knowing they both spit the same meat?"

The crudity was so shocking Dahiya almost gasped; no man of the Amazigh ever spoke to a woman thus, and particularly not one who was the daughter of Tabat.

But the gleam in Aksil's eye told her that reaction was precisely what he was expecting, what he was hoping for. Dahiya would not give it to him.

"I doubt either Apsimar or Ilyan would allow you to live long enough to give you answer to such a question," she said coldly. "And should you see fit to repeat such an insult, Aksil of the Awraba, I will spit you myself – as I did Yedder."

"Yedder," he repeated, untroubled by the threat. "That is where this all began, Dahiya, is it not? With a wrong done to you – and with your revenge." He nodded. "The tale is legend in Carthage. I confess I was myself impressed when I heard it; yes, and impressed that you did not boast of it when we met. I do not question your bravery, Dahiya, and I applaud the manner in which you took vengeance. It was your right."

He leaned closer, and the geniality was quite gone from his tone when he spoke again. "But slicing a man when he thinks himself safe in his bed is not war, Dahiya. Seducing the governor of Septem is not war. And as for lying with the Greek commander" – he shook his head as he held her eyes – "well, Dahiya, the men beyond this tent have a name for such women. A name I would not wish you to be known by. They already suspect what I know to be true. One word from me, and your leadership is gone forever. Any respect they have for you will disappear. You will be no more than the whore who was raped by the Ifren and who took a foreigner to her bed. Any child you have will be tainted. You will have no tent, no adwwar, no kel. You will be a woman with no pride, lost to the sands, wandering aimlessly. What use will your helmet and your sword be then, Dahiya? Do you think they will comfort you when you lie alone on the hard ground, far from any man's fire?"

Dahiya had not moved her eyes from his face as he spoke. She waited until he sat back, eyeing her with the satisfied expression of a man certain his words had achieved the desired effect.

"What would you have me do, Aksil?" she asked, keeping her voice carefully neutral.

He nodded, as if her capitulation was no more than he had expected.

"Command your men to follow me." He was all efficiency now, any trace of rancour gone. "Tell Apsimar you bow to my judgement and that your sword is mine to command, your men allies of the Awraba under my lead. Ask him to fight at my side, under my direction."

"And if I do this?" she asked politely. "What will you give in exchange?"

"I will keep your secret." The hard gleam was back in his eyes. "One of my men saw you, Dahiya. I will have him killed rather than allow him to repeat what he told me – that the Greek took you up against the stone like the most common whore. I will ensure none ever know what you have done. You can keep your father's sword and the ridiculous mask you carry." He dismissed the helmet contemptuously. "Men will still hail you as Tabat's daughter. You can choose any husband you wish – every man here would be proud to have such a wife as you – and make him amgar of Kel Jerawa. Ride at his side, if you choose. None will question the parentage of your sons, nor your right to carry your father's legacy with you. You will still rule, Dahiya, with honour."

"And all this," Dahiya said, "I will do because I fear men will judge me for taking what any of them take, every day, without ever giving thought to reprisal."

"They are men." Aksil shook his head impatiently. "It is different, Dahiya, and you know it."

"I know it."

When Dahiya spoke next, her tone was clear and strong.

"I will ask that Apsimar and the Jerawa follow you, Aksil. I will do so because you are a proven warrior of great experience, one I know Ilyan trusts and whom men will follow. I, too, trust your judgement. I will lead my men into battle behind you with pride. I will do all of this not because I fear you exposing me, Aksil, for all men must decide for themselves what road they choose on their way to greatness, and none may alter the course another man has chosen. I, too, have chosen my path, and I will not hang my head in shame for the choice, but walk where it takes me and face what it brings."

She stood without waiting for him to dismiss her. "When I walk from this tent," she said softly, "you have a choice. You can raise your sword to the men I lead and thank them for riding far from their women to join battle against the Arabic invaders. You can ignore me, for I am no more than a sword, and I do not require your acknowledgment nor your approbation. For every man out there" – she gestured beyond the tent – "my seat in here at your side is confirmation enough that you accept me as amgar. No more need be said. The Jerawa have kneeled to me and given their swords. Unless, and until, I prove unworthy of that allegiance, nothing need change. Or" – she gave him a hard look – "you can walk from here and denounce me as whore, an insult no man allied to my father will ever accept. You can watch Apsimar walk from here, taking his men with him – if he has not killed you already. You can explain to Ilyan why the alliance he has spent time and coin to establish was destroyed in less than a day – merely because your own pride could not accept the fealty of a woman."

She did not try to hide the contempt in her last words. Aksil stood, his face red with anger.

"If you lead men onto that field," he spat, "you will die, Dahiya – and so will they."

"Then you will have what you wish for," said Dahiya calmly, "and I will have given my life for Altava – which is my right, Aksil, as it is the right of every man here."

She turned to leave, and he grasped her arm, his fingers digging into her skin. She did not turn.

"Marry me," he hissed. "Marry me and we will unite Awraba and Jerawa. We will be the greatest *amenokal* in a lifetime – and you will be honoured as Tin Hinan once was. Our sons" – his voice choked with excitement – "our sons will rule Altava, Dahiya. They will be as our kings of old once were."

Dahiya turned. His eyes were dark with ambition and, she realised, with desire. Aksil wanted her; it was not only for politics that he had made this scene.

"I honour you, Aksil," she said quietly. "I honour you as the Leopard you are named for, and for the victories you have brought our people. I honour the sons you will father and the battles you will yet win. I give you my sword and my allegiance, and I offer the Jerawa to you to command. But I will lead them myself. And I will never marry you, Aksil."

She held his eyes until she saw the eagerness there fade.

Then she held open the tent and stepped back respectfully for him to pass.

When they emerged, Dahiya stood behind Aksil, her sword tip on the ground, amongst the other kel leaders. None questioned her, and nor did Aksil mention her by name.

Dahiya kept her eyes to the ground so none could see her triumph – or sense her crippling terror.

16

PRIDE

*All power lies in submission, for what can bend will never break. To bend, we
find the rigid steel of pride and meld it with humility, a living energy both
malleable and resilient, as one tempers iron to steel. Those who wield the crude
metal of pride before them will never know a true sword's strength, but only the
brittle and broken shards of their arrogant dreams.*

The Lady of Aurariola, to her granddaughters
Al Andalus, AD 752

Uqba ibn Nafi had captured the port of Barca twenty years
before. Despite being recalled to Damascus often in the
intervening decades, he had not relinquished his ambi-
tions for Africa. When he had returned, at the head of an army of
ten thousand, he had marched them ruthlessly across the desert
making strategic posts as he went, building a supply line that
stretched from Egypt to Tripolitana, serviced by the steadily
growing fleet of his caliph, Muawiyah.

Kairouan, though, was more than a post. It was a fortified port
that gave the Arabs a toehold on Dahiya's homeland that even the

weakening Greek forces could not ignore. The ships and armies of the caliph had forced the Greek emperor to take the war between their two burgeoning empires into many theatres, from the mountains of Anatolia to the walls of Constantinople itself. Now they found themselves forced to defend their last, fragile hold on the Ifriquiyan lands that had once been jewels of the now-splintered Roman Empire. Those last bastions were weak and ill defended – but even pressed from every side as Emperor Constantine IV was, he knew he could not afford to lose any more ports to the caliph's growing fleet. To this end, he had dispatched a large force of the newly formed *Karabisianoi*, a fleet constructed from the old imperial naval themes, to the shores of Africa, with instructions to hold the ports there at any cost. The *Karabisianoi* had been built to go where the emperor required it and fight on any shore. It was a swift, lethal, and effective force and, with hardened warriors such as Apsimar and his brother Heraclius leading detachments, had succeeded in at least meeting the Arabs as their naval forces grew.

The men of the *Karabisianoi* were accustomed to not only rowing great distances and fighting at sea but also leaving their dromons on the shore and marching far into the interior. They often formed scouting parties that went into places even the most hardened of the emperor's forces might think twice about entering. The force that joined the ranks of the Amazigh now were men of exactly such valour – hardened and battle scarred, accustomed to living on nothing and marching far into the unknown. They faced the coming battle with the calm, humorous stoicism of men accustomed to facing death and unafraid at the prospect of it. The Arabic armies were nothing new to them. They had faced them in the mountains of Anatolia and the plains of Thessalonica, and they knew well the tactics they might face.

"But," said Aksil, as they sat in council that night, "you have not faced them on the hard, arid plains to the south-west of Kairouan, where the sand becomes mountains and a man is easily lost. We know this ground like no other. No man might match us on it."

His men murmured their approval. Dahiya, sitting quietly with her tagelmust shielding her eyes, watched them as he spoke.

"Uqba ibn Nafi is no stranger to desert," Apsimar said. "He has fought his way across this one. None have been able to halt his progress – not the kels to the east, who came at his forces over and over on the coast, in the mountains, and in the sands; not our own forces, which have tried to wrest control of Barca from his grasp multiple times. Do not underestimate him, Cæcilius. Uqba is a hard man and a brilliant strategist."

Dahiya had to discipline herself not to curl her lip at Apsimar's use of the Latin name Aksil had affected since allying himself with the Greeks. She found Aksil's adoption of the name "Cæcilius" an insulting, pathetic attempt at insinuation with men who would only ever see him as a savage. Dahiya did not understand why anyone would wish to be other than exactly what they were: proud Imazighen, free men of the sands. She was not alone; the other Amazigh leaders addressed him as Aksil, looking pointedly away when the Greek commanders addressed him by his new epithet.

Dahiya watched Aksil surreptitiously as he talked strategy with the Greeks, whilst his Imazighen advisors watched on from behind their indigo veils. *He wants their approval*, she thought. *Aksil sees their dromons and their order, the great fortresses they still command, and he wants a seat at their table. He wants what Ilyan has: territory to govern, taxes to collect, and the honours bestowed by a distant authority. He may speak of Altava, but he does not believe – not truly. For Aksil, the only way he imagines rule is that of a surrogate, an inferior to a greater power.*

But Aksil, Dahiya knew, did not have Ilyan's wily cunning. Ilyan may have governed under the aegis of Constantinople, but he corresponded with the Goths of Spania, and the Franks further to the north, and named them allies. He paid no taxes to Greece and had no standing army. Ilyan ruled by a fragile web of alliances, holding the port of Septem by guile, trade, and information. Greece would send troops to protect it when the emperor thought it in his interests, as it was now, with Uqba's forces threatening the sea routes that guaranteed trade to the eastern capital. But all knew that Ilyan's port stood because of Ilyan himself. Aksil had neither the diplomacy nor the patience to cultivate men as Ilyan did. Aksil was a warrior of the desert. He had made his name in the wars between kels, judging his own success by the camels he held and the wealth of his adwwar. Aksil did not think of foreign kings and their politics, nor of the greater movement of humanity and trade over the Circle of Lands. He thought of coin, palace, and men bowing before his superiority. He had neither the vision to create a nation such as the Altava of Dahiya's imagination nor the intelligence to rule it if he did.

Do I? Dahiya wondered, allowing the talk of battle and strategy to flow over her. *Am I truly able to envisage that nation – and believe myself capable of ruling it?*

It was a different thing, she mused, to contemplate a fantasy than to plan for its execution. And yet, she knew, Altava was her destiny. She would create it – or she would die defending the idea of it. But Aksil's way – that, Dahiya knew, was not a compromise she was capable of accepting.

"And the Jerawa?" It was Igider's voice that broke through her reverie. Dahiya looked up to find her clansman staring fixedly at Aksil, his anger visible in the stiff-jawed manner of his question. "We are the next largest clan to your own, Aksil, to come to this battle. And yet thus far, I have heard nothing of where our position is to be in this battle of yours. One might imagine we are not present at all."

Thinking of her musings of only a moment ago, Dahiya smiled wryly to herself. *Before Altava,* she thought resignedly, *I must fight the battle of my sex.*

"We will fight as Cæcilius orders," she said clearly, the stern countenance she turned to Igider brooking no opposition. "In this battle, we serve our leader and the strategy he determines."

Clearly gratified by her use of his Latin name, and equally surprised by her unexpected advocacy, Aksil nodded magnanimously at her. "You are Tabat's daughter, indeed," he said graciously. "Perhaps, Dahiya of the Jerawa, you might give us your council as to how best your men might serve on the field?"

Dahiya nodded respectfully, acknowledging his generosity with a courtesy she did not feel. She knew the Jerawa were being punished for having her as a leader. It was petty, and counterproductive, but fighting it would achieve nothing.

"We have a herd of horses," she said quietly, "trained beyond anything I have seen before – horses from Illiberis, across the sea, in Spania."

A low murmuring broke out. The horses of Illiberis were not unknown to the Imazighen Riders, though, just as Dahiya herself, most had thought them a myth, or at least a story embellished for children.

"I suggest we come at the Arabic forces from the rear," Dahiya said. "Keep us away from your front lines; do not allow the Arabs to know we exist. We can disappear into the earth and remain hidden until the Arabs truly believe themselves the victors. Then we will ride upon their rear guard, our bowmen atop the horses, raining them with a hail of arrows they will be unable to defend against."

Men had begun muttering at her first words. By the time she finished speaking there was a cacophony of voices, none of them complimentary; even Dahiya's own men looked at the ground in shame. It was unheard of for a warrior of the Amazigh to ask to remain out of the line of attack, and even worse to request an attack by stealth. It was not their way.

"It is not honourable," muttered Igider, winding his turban with agitated movements and staring to the side.

Aksil could not hide his own smirk. "Indeed," he said, not bothering to conceal his contempt, "it is a plan I would expect of a woman, Dahiya." He shrugged. "I can see no objection to it," he said carelessly. "With the Awraba and the Greek forces at the forefront, there will be little left to do on the ground but murder those who flee, but this, I accept, is a job for women rather than men."

The other leaders held their veils across their faces and looked away, unwilling to offer such direct insult to their Jerawa brothers. Zdan looked stolidly at the ground before him. Apsimar, opposite her, wore an expression of grim anger, but he would not, she knew, interrupt such a conversation, although he understood what she planned where Aksil did not. Apsimar knew she was not there to cut down fleeing men, saw behind her words to an intention Aksil was too blind and arrogant to either see or accept if it was pointed out to him.

Apsimar, though, was not amongst them to command their forces, but rather to aid them with his own. Whilst Aksil would ultimately work with him, it did not serve Apsimar to contradict him in front of the *amenokal*. Apsimar was too smart a strategist to make such a mistake.

He also knew, as she did, that to come to her defence would be to claim her as his woman – and curse her leadership to the sands.

"And you, Dahiya?" said Aksil, the sneer barely masked in his tone. "What men will you send to the field to do this work?"

"I have already told you, Aksil, that I will lead the men myself," said Dahiya quietly. "It is I who have trained with the horses, teaching my Riders the patterns and timing required to achieve the effect I wish for. I am amgar of the Jerawa. I will ride at their forefront."

If the men had muttered before, now their astonishment was palpable, some actually leaping to their feet in a breach of etiquette customarily unthinkable in the sedate surrounds of the council tent. Despite the fact that they had already played out this farce in this same tent only days before, Aksil could not resist the opportunity to play it again, this time to a willing crowd.

"You," said Aksil, his body shaking with laughter. "You, Dahiya? A girl who has never so much as led men against another kel – you would ride into battle waving Ahar, leading warriors twice your age against an experienced army?" He shook his head. "I knew you for an upstart, Dahiya," he said softly. "But I had not thought you a fool. You will die – and your men with you."

"Then I will die, Aksil, as I told you the last time we had this conversation." Winding her tagelmust about her face, she stood and faced the shocked expressions that looked at her with everything from pity to contempt.

"You will tell me where you plan to face them," she said calmly, "and give me a day to find shelter before you do. The Jerawa will do the rest."

She did not wait for their response but turned and left the tent, aware of Zdan and Igider, heads bowed in shame, following her.

She did not look at Apsimar. She had seen the doubt that lurked behind his eyes. She could not bear to see his attempts to hide it.

17

———

FEAR

*You might climb the tallest tree and never fear the fall. But should your child set
one foot upon the branch, fear will strike the deepest chord within. Never is fear
greater than when it is not for ourselves, but for those we love. In war it is the
same: whilst we must know ourselves invincible to ride to war, we learn our
fallibility through trembling at the vulnerability of others.*

The Lady of Aurariola, to her granddaughters
Al Andalus, AD 752

Dahiya was barely out of earshot of the tent when Igider
exploded.

"Attacking from the rear? After the work of battle has
been done, you offer the Jerawa, the finest fighters of all the
Amazigh, as a cowardly run from behind?" He grasped Dahiya's
arm, forcibly turning her to face him. "I did not name you amgar
for this," he spat. "I did not speak for you, and follow you, to bring
shame to my ancestors and my kel, to send other men to do work
that is my own destiny."

109

Zdan stared woodenly at the ground, but his very silence was deafening in its condemnation.

Dahiya waited until he had finished. Igider gave her arm an angry shake and stood back.

"Before the Ifren attacked," she said calmly, "do you recall the mission upon which my father had been engaged?"

"Barely," Igider threw back. "I was busy, you might recall, fighting against the same Arab bastards you now wish me to run from."

"In a small group," Dahiya pointed out. "Small attacks, at different points along the Arab lines. Do you recall what the main purpose of those attacks was?"

Igider frowned. "Tabat wanted us to enter their camps at night," he said. "To discover their numbers, and then to terrify them. Burn their stores and take their animals." He bared his teeth in a fierce smile. "Which," he said grimly, "we did."

"To discover their numbers." Dahiya nodded. "And as you know, my father sent men not just to one part of the Arab lines. He sent groups to harry every part of their force. Every camp, every detachment, for a thousand miles and more, my father sent men to inspect − yes, to terrify, and burn, and harass. But mostly to learn. And then he sent word to Ilyan, in Septem, and made plans to meet with him. Why do you think he did that, Igider?"

Igider's eyes narrowed, but he did not reply. Zdan, too, was looking at her now, his interest sharpened.

"Because my father discovered something very important in these forays into Arabic territory." Dahiya met their eyes. "He discovered that the Arabs are too many for us to meet in pitched battle. Even with the Greek forces at our backs and in an *amenokal*, a confederation of the clans. Even if every single one of the clans fought together, still, my father knew, we would not be enough."

Igider gave a contemptuous snort. "Tabat of the Jerawa would not have allowed that to stop him."

"No," Dahiya agreed mildly. "He most certainly would not − just as I will not. But nor was he a fool who valued the lives of his men so lightly he would send them mindlessly to slaughter, as Aksil seems so eager to do." She held up a hand to forestall Igider's indignation. "Spare me your posturing," she said, and there was now nothing mild in her tone. "My father knew men. He knew Aksil. The reason he went to Septem was because he respected Ilyan and knew he would listen to my father's plan from an objective position, rather than through the dubious veil of his own pride – which is the window through which Aksil assesses every decision he makes. My father did not think of how glorious the Jerawa might look riding at the head of a Greek horde, as if we command them – which any man of sense knows we do not and cannot. He thought instead of how we could fight – and win. And he discussed those plans with me, his daughter. He explained them in detail. Why do you think," she went on, staring between them in turn, "I have spent these past weeks drilling our men, every day, for hours after we cease marching, in formation with bow and arrow? Did you think it was a game, or that I simply enjoyed watching the Illiberis horses go through their paces?"

Neither man answered her. They were listening now, with dawning awareness on their faces.

"Aksil's assault will fail." Dahiya spoke in a low tone, for it would not do to say such things in the hearing of other men. "The Arabs will let him come. They will meet him on the plains beyond Kairouan, and for a time, they will allow him to win. Perhaps, he may even defeat their central force. But he will lose, and his men will die."

Zdan was watching her intently. "Then what is it," he said, "that you plan to do?"

"I will explain my strategy to you, and you will ensure men follow my orders." Dahiya glanced around warily. "Walk with me," she said, "and I will tell you."

* * *

THE SKY WAS INDIGO when Dahiya finally made her way back into camp. She was exhausted, but exhilarated too. Now her plan could begin – and so could the future of her people.

"Dahiya."

She spun around, her hand on Ahar, but it was reflex, nothing

III

more. She had known who it would be from the moment he opened his mouth.

"We should not talk here," she said softly, glancing around.

"Then we will go far into the desert," said Apsimar grimly, "where we can yell instead."

She sighed mentally and allowed him to lead her away from the camp, into the high cliffs. He walked until the camp was no more than a vague smudge in the distance and he was sure no man had followed them, then he rounded on Dahiya and seized her shoulders hard enough to leave marks, shaking her with a fury she had not thought him capable of with her.

"When we spoke with Ilyan," he ground out, "when you shared your plans, never once did you explain yourself fully. Even later — when you could have told me, said something — still, you allowed me to believe you would be present at the battle, not at the head of your own. Dahiya, you do not know what you do. None of them" — he flung out a furious arm, encompassing Aksil, his own men, the entire camp — "not one of those fools has half an idea what you have planned. Aksil thinks you await his orders, not that you run your own battle. If any of them knew, they would tear you to pieces as a traitor — and I would understand their anger, Dahiya, for your very plan rests upon your assumption of their defeat. Is it not enough that you are the architect of this madness without also needing to be its martyr?"

The rage had faded from his voice as he spoke, his grip upon her calming, until his words were more plea than fury, his large hands cradling rather than hurting.

"You think you know what it will be," he said hoarsely, "the moment you turn your horse into that insane mass. You think it will be blood and exhilaration and glory, you atop your warhorse, controlling your men as you do on the drill ground of an afternoon. Precision and technique. Careful shooting at planned targets. But you know nothing of the reality, Dahiya. You do not know the shit and piss and stench of it, the screams of men as they die and the chaos that takes all you are and turns you once again into a child waking to a nightmare, helpless and terrified and doing anything you can to simply live. You do not know it, and Dahiya — *Xristus*,

Daya − I swear I cannot watch you learn. You might lead the men in name." He touched her face. "But you cannot lead them to battle, and men will not follow you there."

"And you?" Dahiya answered him quietly. "Would you lead your men, Apsimar, to the edge of a battle, only to send them in before you and remain at the rear, calling useless orders and praying to your Xristus that they are followed? Could you do such a thing, Apsimar, and still call yourself man?"

"But you are not man," said Apsimar roughly, cradling her face in his hands. "You are not, Daya, no matter that you are the bravest woman I have ever met. No matter that already you have done more than most men could have with what you have endured. But you are not a man, Daya. And you are not ready for this."

"Were you?" she countered, and she felt the rage rise within her, saw the moment when he, too, saw it in her eyes and stepped back, his hands falling away. "Were you ready, the first time your dromon sailed into battle, Apsimar? Were you ready the first time your sword slid through another man's heart and you felt his lifeblood fall from it? Tell me, Apsimar: do you think any of us, ever, are ready for that?"

"It is different," he muttered, his mouth a tight, angry line.

"No!" She cut him off. "No, Apsimar, it is not different. I am not a man. But I have ridden with men all my life. I carried a sword before I did a cooking pot. I carved my own bow when the branch was taller than I myself. I rode with men and I watched them ride to war like scared children, bathing their wounds when they returned with blank eyes and shaking hands. I heard their screams in the night. I buried those who did not return alive. I learned from those who did. I practised in the afternoons when other men slept, and I was knocked to the ground more times than any boy who trained with me. I learned that a woman must fight a different way if she is to disarm a man. I learned that a woman must be smarter than any single one of her rivals, for not only must she win the battle of steel and bow, but she must also fight her own men − for respect, for loyalty, even simply to be considered a voice worth hearing. But I learned another thing, too, Apsimar." She stepped closer to him, feeling the pulse that ran between them like a live thing between her legs, feeling herself crave him already.

"I learned that every man underestimates a woman," she said softly. "That no man can bear to think a woman might be smarter than him, or faster, or – the gods forbid – stronger. And in that, Apsimar, lies my power – and my magic." She reached out a hand and put it against his chest, feeling the harsh thud of his heart like thunder against her skin. "I did not think," she whispered, "that I would find you to be that man. Are you, Apsimar? Are you a man who cannot accept a woman as his equal – and allow her to do what she must?"

For a moment, she thought she had him, thought he would take her and groan against her mouth and plunge within her as she longed for him to do. For a moment, his mouth opened close to hers, and she swayed toward him, already surrendering.

Then the air shifted, and her eyes flew open to find him standing away from her, his breath harsh in his chest, his face taut with pain and rage.

"I *am* a man," he said roughly. "Xristus help me, Daya – I am a man who is in love with you. And if you think such a man can watch his woman ride to her own death and do nothing to intervene, then you know less of men than you think you do – and nothing of me at all."

He stared at her in the darkness for a long, pained moment, during which she felt him withdraw from her, felt him take away the current that had sustained her every day since first they met, the pulse that had lived beneath her skin and in her heart and which, even now, grew a new life inside of her.

And then Apsimar turned and walked away, and Dahiya of the Jerawa stood in the silent desert night, as alone and bereft as ever she had been.

18

BATTLE

I wonder what the Arabs felt, that first time they met her in battle. They do not write of it. I have heard the stories from the Amazigh, who exaggerate it as all people do their heroic tales. But I wonder still about that first day, before the legend spread and men learned to fear her. If the gods grant me any vision when I cross the final river to death, it would be to know that: what her enemies felt when they realised what rode at them across the sands the day Dahiya of the Jerawa took the field.

The Lady of Aurariola, to her granddaughters
Al Andalus, AD 752

The dawn came in a red haze that turned the cliffs to blood. Dahiya woke from a restless dream, into which she had slipped just before dawn after a wide-eyed, heart-pounding night. Her stomach churned, and her mouth felt sour.

The coming battle seemed nothing to Apsimar's remote expression as they had parted. Dahiya felt numb, inured to the coming horrors as cleanly as if she were drunk.

115

Does it matter? she thought. *This battle, death, Altava. Does any of it matter, to me, if I do not have him?*

She knew the shame of such thoughts. Knew they were not worthy of Tabat's daughter, especially not as she faced her first battle.

And yet the treacherous thoughts remained.

Dahiya stared out over the barren plain below, upon which men would soon die.

I should not care, she thought dully. *Nothing should matter more than this.*

Dahiya could not recall a time in her life when Altava had not been her objective. Could not think of a moment when she had considered betraying the vision of her father, the dream upon which her life had been built.

Yet now she stood on the precipice of destiny, the day when she might emerge from her father's shadow to become what she had always, in her heart, known she could be – and as if she were no more than the silliest of the adwwar girls, all Dahiya could think of was Apsimar and of the expression on his face as he had stepped away from her.

She touched her belly, and the wind whispered in her father's voice: *It is time you ceased dreaming of carrying the Lion into battle, Dahiya, and turned your thoughts instead to the cubs you will carry in your arms…*

Dahiya felt the unaccustomed sting of tears. She swallowed hard and dashed them away with one hand, cursing herself for a fool and her body for weakness.

It is right that I carry my son into battle, she told herself fiercely. *All sons of the desert must learn war in the womb.*

Then she recalled Apsimar's rage, the heat of his body within her own, and shuddered with longing and regret.

Such comforts are not mine to seek, she thought dully. An image rose of Yedder above her, tearing through the barrier of her virginity with brute savagery. *That was my truth,* she thought. *That was my grief – and my power. All else is nothing.*

She thought of Acantha, the woman who had been denied revenge. She thought of the woman in her adwwar who had stared at her in accusation: *The man who took me was named Badis. When he lies suffering on the ground, screaming for his mother, his guts on your sword – then I follow you. Until then, it is just words.*

I fight for them, Dahiya thought. She seized upon the woman's pain, felt in it the memory of her own.

I fight for the pain of injustice done and injustice that will be done. I fight so no woman ever suffers what we have, at the hands of our own men or those of the Arabs. I fight not just for the dream of Altava, but for what I imagine that dream to be.

She touched her belly again, feeling the life she knew lived there.

I fight so that you, my son, become the man women need you to be. And to do that I must be the woman for all, one men can follow and women can love. I must be better than my fears and my weakness. If that means I sacrifice love, then the man is not worth the love I would have given him. I cannot trade my dreams for selfish desire. Too much rests upon them.

But even as she felt the truth run through her, powering her with a force she knew but did not understand, she saw in her mind an image of Apsimar, tall and bronze, readying for battle.

I want you, she thought, sadness and loss mingling with that force to become something else, something true yet also utterly devastating.

My grief is my power.

Dahiya touched Ahar at her side and reached for her bow.

It was time to go to war.

* * *

"They are dying." Igider's voice was low and agonised. "Surely it is time –"

"We wait." Her tone silenced him, but his pain was her own.

Below the cliffs, the Amazigh screamed their fury and defiance, their pride, but they screamed to the wind, dying cries that choked on Arabic steel and fell to the sand in futile red clouds, only to be trampled as more of the enemy poured from the gates and into their midst.

It was worse even than Dahiya had imagined. Uqba had not held back his forces, as she had thought he might. Perhaps it had been the sight of Greek forces arrayed alongside the Amazigh.

117

Perhaps his arrogance lay in the numbers he knew he held behind Kairouan's impregnable walls. Whatever the reason, Uqba had opened the gates soon after dawn, pouring the full fury of his battle-hardened army from them, men who had marched through the barren sands and suffered the nightly terror of a hidden enemy they could neither predict nor prepare for. Men who had faced thirst and the strange song of the sands when the sky darkened and there was nothing but dun-coloured haze and their own fears. Men who had been told a hundred generations of their sons would die before their caliph relinquished his dream of conquest.

Men who fought for a God Dahiya did not know and for a man they believed spoke the words of that God.

Dahiya touched the mask of Ghurzla at her side and felt the odd rush of power within it.

But they do not fight with the gods of this land, she thought fiercely. *They do not fight for their mother, for their heart.*

As she thought it, she saw the front line of the Amazigh falter. She stiffened, forcing herself to wait.

The Greeks in their iron and leather surged inward, then fell back again, like a tide lapping the shore as it ran out. The first of them turned their backs on the Arabic enemy.

A scream of triumph came from the Arabs lining the walls.

Then it was the Amazigh moving backward, men calling out in fear and defeat; the first faltering step became a rush and then a mad stampede.

It is time.

Even as she thought it, the gates opened wide as the Arabs threw all caution to the wind. As she watched, the figures upon the walls began to fall away as the stream of men from the gate became an exuberant flood, the triumphant Arabic army racing on foot onto the plains to wreak their bloody revenge upon the force that had taken so many of their lives in stealth and darkness.

Dahiya's hand tightened on the reins, and her tall black warhorse began to surge and plunge as the power reached him. Wheeling the animal, she dropped the reins and held him with her legs as she raised the heavy, savage helmet. She stared at the men before her in silence, letting them see her, see the woman they had chosen and the leader they doubted still. She stared at them long enough to frustrate, to allow them to truly feel their doubt and know it was she who sat on the horse, she, Dahiya, who was about to lead them into battle against impossible odds. To know, and to never forget.

And then she lowered Ghurzla over her head and felt it, the moment when the blood of her ancestors rushed through her and she became one with the curved horns that touched the sky, one with her past and all those who had known Ghurzla in their blood and his power in their sword. She pulled the tall bow from her back and held it to the sky.

"*Altava!*" she shrieked.

"*Altava!*" the men of the Jerawa roared. "*Altava!*"

And then they poured onto the plain in a torrent of pounding hooves and snarling horseflesh, a thousand men and more guiding their animals with no more than thought and will. Their bows came up as they became two tight concentric circles that flowed into each other like the serpents of the Illiberis brand. They came on in an inexorable hail of arrows, each man releasing five from his hand as he wheeled his horse into the circle and drew another five, whilst more arrows took his place. The relentless shower of death rained down upon the Arabic army, who turned as one man in confusion and growing fear.

Then the Amazigh and Greek forces were turning back, their faces changing as they saw the woman they had dismissed leading a force they had not imagined, howling with renewed fury as they saw the deadly Riders plunge into the fray. The Arabic fear turned to horror as they recognised their mistake and began to rush for their gates and the safety of their walls.

But it was too late, for they found themselves faced with a snarling, horned demon on a great black warhorse, and even as they fell back in superstitious awe, the demon threw down the bow and pulled the great, long war sword, Ahar, and rode, shrieking blood and vengeance, into their midst.

She was no longer Dahiya, and nor was she Ghurzla. She was neither woman nor Jerawa. She was a sword and an arm, a weapon of her father's dream and the land that had spawned her. She was part of a destiny that had existed before she ever did, and a power that belonged to no man or woman but existed in the moment of death alone, and to those fated to live that moment over and over. She felt it flow through her and into the steel and men around her, so the Jerawa became the avenging spear-tip of a ravaging horde, claiming their land, Altava, and their vengeance.

For a time, it seemed they could not prevail. There were men who turned their backs, men who feared still the screams of the Arabic invaders. One of those men turned his face to her as he began to flee. Dahiya saw the fresh scar across his left eye and knew it as the face of the Ifren man, Badis; she shrieked the rage of the woman who had once stood before her in the adwwar, and the long steel of Ahar pierced his guts, spilling them upon the ground.

"Amazigh!" she screamed to those who would dare flee. "For Altava! For death!"

And those who would run felt it, the moment when her fury snatched victory from the jaws of defeat.

They rounded with savage cries of triumph and renewed frenzy, and together they bore down upon the army caught in their pincer, screaming bloodlust as the Arabs died on sands that had never been, and never would be, theirs.

Finally the great gates were dragged closed, even as Amazigh swords pounded upon them. The tattered remnants of the Arab army lining the walls stared down at the plain.

Amidst their dead, the horned demon rode astride a blood-stained horse of ebony black, raised sword dripping with gore as men screamed their approbation.

Wheeling the animal to face the walls, the demon's head went back, and an unearthly shriek echoed from the cliffs.

The men on the walls shuddered in fear and terror. They knew that it was no man who had defeated their hitherto unconquered force, but something else, something they could neither fight nor understand.

Then the great helmet came off, and a long, rippling sea of black hair cascaded down to touch the horse's flanks, the one indistinguishable from the other, and the watching men gasped in shock and awe as the demon was revealed as a girl child no older than their own daughters, a woman who spun her horse with her legs and screamed her rage and defiance at the men she had just defeated, accepting the roars of her own people as they claimed her.

"A sorceress," muttered one of the Arabs on the walls, and the words spread like wildfire from mouth to mouth as men recognised they had been defeated not by human hand but by the sorcery of a demon woman, and they began to call the witch by her name from the walls.

"Al Kahinat!" they cried. "The Sorceress!"

"Al Kahinat! Al Kahinat…"

Far below, on the bloody plains, the sound reached the Imazighen, and they laughed in exultation as the meaning of the name spread between them. Their swords came up, and they hailed the new amgar in their midst and called her by the name men call that which they can never understand in woman:

Sorceress.

Al Kahinat, Queen of the Jerawa, spun her horse amongst her men and knew herself for the first time.

19

DAHIYA

*Players come now to your father's hall, singing songs of our wars. I sit in our gards, here on the soil that was once Mater Spania, and listen to them sing of battles I saw, some in which I swung steel of my own. They do not sing my name, and they rarely sing of Dahiya. They do not sing the lost name of Illiberis, nor of the magic in the caves there, just as they do not sing of Dahiya's red rocks and the visions she knew. War is told by men, my daughters, and claimed by them. They will tell you that no woman can fight as men do. They will teach you to be what men want women to be. But know this, my beautiful children: you are women, and women are strong. You will face battles, some chosen, some not. I cannot fight them for you, and nor can I teach you how they are to be fought. I can tell you only to know the strength within you, to trust it —
and to always bend, never break.*

The Lady of Aurariola, to her granddaughters
Al Andalus, AD 752

The men were feasting, but Dahiya could not join them.

She knew men after battle. Knew the wild drinking and mindless lust. Their company was no place for any woman, even one whom they claimed as their own.

Dahiya was as alone in her triumph as ever she had been.

They had hailed her, and for that she was grateful. Aksil had led his army, and he had triumphed, but the victory, all knew, belonged to Dahiya. Aksil himself had curtly acknowledged as much, for he could do little else, and men expected it. Dahiya had accepted it, then ridden from the field and away from the jubilation of victory, for Aksil's approbation had been given reluctantly. She knew today was but the beginning of a long and difficult road, one that she and Aksil must learn to travel together. For now, they had what she had come for. The Amazigh had a victory, and Dahiya had her place at the head of the Jerawa.

It was a beginning.

She strode deep into the sands, away from the sounds of men. She carried a guerba and clean robes. When she was far from any sounds, she stripped down and washed away the dirt and death from her skin, naked beneath the desert night as the empty wind dried her body.

Dahiya heard him coming, as she had known he would.

She stood bare beneath the stars, waiting, and heard the sharp intake of his breath as he saw her.

"I carry your child," she said, without preamble. "He will be a warrior. Today he tasted victory in his mother's blood." She touched her belly, her eyes on Apsimar's face.

"I cannot be the wife you have in your home," Dahiya said quietly. "I am not a woman of the adwwar, to welcome your return after your victories and tend your wounds when you are ill. I will carry scars of my own" – she touched an angry red line on her arm, others on her legs – "and perhaps, one day, I will die on the field, for it is often thus for those who lead men."

She stepped forward haltingly, trying to find the words that were the hardest for her.

"I told you once," she whispered, coming closer to his still face, "that I needed you. I do, Apsimar; I need you more than the victory or the name amgar. I need you more than the men I lead or the land to which I am bound. I need you like the air I breathe."

She reached out a hand and touched the hard planes of his face, feeling him tremble slightly.

"Do not ask me to choose," she whispered, turning her face

upward as she reached him. "Do not force me to betray one part of myself in order to have another."

He moved then, his hands cradling her face. She placed her own over them, and their fingers entwined as he leaned his forehead to hers. They breathed the same air, in and out.

Finally he spoke.

"Today I saw a legend born."

His thumbs stroked the high cheekbones. "A legend men will sing of down the passage of years, with fear and awe – and respect." His hands, still entwined with hers, slid down her body to the faint swell of her belly and rested there. "A legend," he said huskily, "for our sons to be proud of."

He kissed her then, deep and long, his touch telling her what no words could: that he knew her for the woman she was and loved her for it, just as he admired the legend she would become.

"You are not afraid," she murmured as they drew apart. "You are not afraid of me."

"Dahiya." He stroked the hair away from her face and shook his head. "You terrify me more than any person alive or dead." He gave her a twisted smile. "But my fear has nothing to do with Al Kahinat, no matter the magic she may wield." His wry tone told her he knew the spell she had wrought, knew the conscious theatre she had built to take her power.

"Then what?" she whispered.

"This." He took her mouth again, hot and hungry this time, and when they parted her breath came short and her naked body arched toward his own, feeling the rough scrape of leather and steel against her skin like a thrill.

"I fear this," he said hoarsely, pulling her against him. "I fear the longing I have for you and the terror of leaving you. I fear watching you do what I know you must and my inability to alter it. I fear that I will not be strong enough to sail from these shores knowing you remain fighting upon them." He held her face so she saw the naked truth of his soul in his eyes, and she knew herself safe to be lost in them.

"I will never force you to choose," he said roughly. "I will never ask of you what I could not myself do. But I do not know how to live with it."

"When you sail from here, you leave my world. Perhaps you will return to it. Perhaps not." Dahiya held his eyes. "Your son may never know the touch of his father's hand. But I will raise him to honour you." She put her hand between his chest and hers, the beat of their bodies flowing as one through her palm. "You will live in me, as I will live in you, and like this we will live together, no matter how far, or long, we are apart."

"How can it be enough, Dahiya?" He cradled her face, and she felt herself open to his touch as she did to his heart.

"There is no such thing as enough," she whispered, reaching for him beneath the high stars of the desert night. "There is only what we have, and the moment in which we have it." She gripped his face fiercely. "In this moment, Apsimar, I know myself the most fortunate woman to walk the earth – and in that I will find my enough."

He held her face, staring at the reflection of the desert sky in her eyes.

"Al Kahinat might be the Sorceress from whom men flee." He pulled her roughly to him. "But no matter how many wars she wins – it will always be you, Dahiya, that I crave."

"Will it be enough?"

A half smile twisted his face.

"We are creatures of war, Dahiya."

His arms tightened and she felt the desert fall around them, shielding their love from the world beyond.

"We will make it enough."

20

AL KAHINAT

I am tired now, and the shadows grow long. Another day, when the men are far from home and we are alone, I will tell you of the votive crown of Spania, for that is our story, your story, and the beginning of the world in which you live. There are women in that story just as fierce as Dahiya, though they fought battles she would not recognise, against foes more cunning than steel on a field. Go, now, but remember who you are. Born of Aurariola's sons you might be — but you are mine, too. Daughters of Illiberis, as I am. In you runs the blood of the horse and the magic of the caves. Use your power wisely, my beautiful girls. Use it well.

The Lady of Aurariola, to her granddaughters
Al Andalus, AD 752

Ilyan, Count of Septem, leaned forward, his eyes bright with interest.

"Is there more?" he asked, pouring wine for the messenger.

The man shrugged. "They say Al Kahinat rides now at the head

126

of her own force, attacking every camp the Arabs have made and burning them to the ground."

"Aksil?"

"He leads an army bigger than any previous alliance. He is a good leader, and men follow him willingly. He has harried Uqba's forces mercilessly, but the Arab is no fool. He has not met him in open battle again. For now, the conflict plays out in small skirmishes amongst the sands, and Uqba continues to claim victories along the coast."

Ilyan stood abruptly and twitched his robes behind his back. He strode across the marble floor – one, two, three, four, five – turned and paced back. He did this a number of times, then stopped and spun, fixing the messenger with so piercing a gaze that the man started in shock.

"Apsimar has gone," he said. It was a statement, not a question, and the man looked confused as he nodded.

"Yes. The fleet sailed some time ago, though it will return. It must. The Greeks will not see Carthage fall to Uqba."

Ilyan snorted. "The Greeks will not save Carthage. That will be our work. Work I do not intend to leave for fate." He stared into the distance, his mind working the multiple pathways it always did. "We will need more even than Al Kahinat and Aksil," he said, speaking to himself more than his audience. "We will need every ally we can make, from here to Francia if needs must." He frowned, remembering something.

"The Goth," he said abruptly. "The brother to the Spanish king."

"Giscila." The messenger nodded.

"Where is he now?"

"He sails the coast, robbing merchant dromons. Nothing too serious: a shipment here, a chest of coin there. He is a nuisance, no more."

"Watch him," said Ilyan. "I would not wish for such a man to fall from sight."

"Should I contrive to have him go missing?"

Ilyan paused for a moment, considering. "No," he said finally. "He may prove useful."

The man nodded and waited.

"Spania," said Ilyan eventually.

The messenger looked up in surprise. "What of it?"

"If Africa falls," said Ilyan, "Spania will be next. It is perhaps time to speak to those men of Spania who might listen to such a warning."

"The Gothic kings are not known for their interest in our affairs," said the man dryly. "Their nobles squabble amongst themselves for land, and their church gains more power with every passing day. Their Jews arrive on our shores, exiled and impoverished. The Goths mistrust us for taking them. They are unlikely to aid us."

"Then we must use our coin to persuade the Gothic king otherwise." Ilyan nodded decisively. "We will begin to make alliances, find those in Spania with whom we might work."

The messenger nodded his acceptance, trying to hide his scepticism.

"You may go," said Ilyan, turning away, his thoughts already elsewhere.

The man had reached the door when Ilyan's voice halted him.

"Al Kahinat."

The messenger turned to find Ilyan staring out of the arched window at something the messenger could not see, robes bunched in his hands behind him.

"I heard," Ilyan said carefully, "that she had a son."

The messenger stared at his back.

"It is true," he said. "Men say the child is the Greek commander's. She carries another in her belly now – a parting gift, they say, from Apsimar."

He saw something stiffen in Ilyan's body.

"Men do not say it to her face," the messenger added quickly. "She has never spoken of who fathered her sons, and none dare ask." He swallowed, a nervous gesture, and lowered his voice in the manner men did when they spoke of the woman the Arabs called Sorceress.

"Al Kahinat, they say, has earned the right to name her sons as she pleases and take her pleasure where she may."

Ilyan looked out through the carved stone arch to the distant plains, which spread south and became harder and more arid until eventually becoming the golden sands upon which even now Dahiya of the Jerawa carved her legend.

He saw her as first he had, standing by a well in the afternoon sun, so tall and proud and beautiful he had thought his heart would break at the sight.

He smiled, a grim, thin line of regret that no man would ever see.

"Good," he said curtly.

"Good."

AL KAHINAT'S AMENOKAL

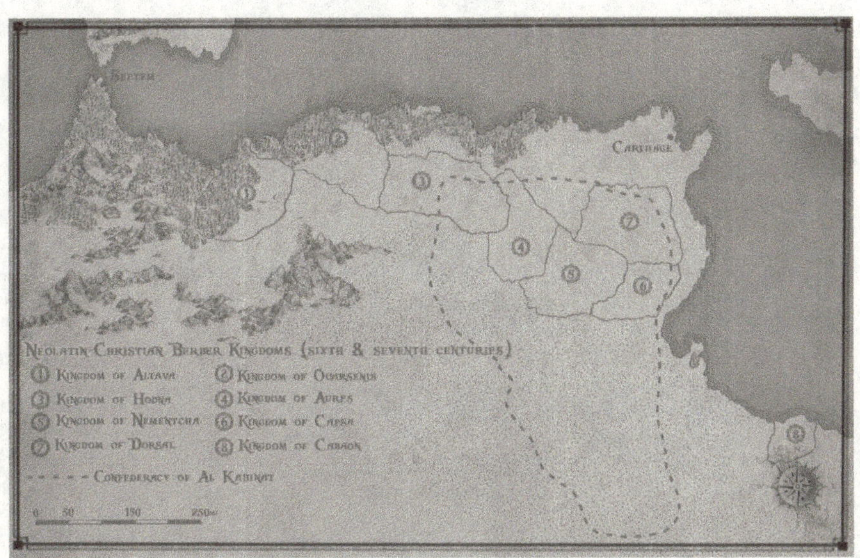

AFTERWORD

Paula Constant, Sahara, Mali 2005

To read the opening chapters of book one in the Visigoths of Spain series, The Votive Crown, please go to:

http://www.paulaconstant.com/the-votive-crown

Thankyou for sharing Dahiya's journey. I fell in love with her story when I walked across the Sahara with my own camels, back in 2005-6. I have always wanted to tell it. Even though she does play an important role in the Visigoths of Spain series, I wanted to do her backstory justice with a dedicated work. I first heard her story told around a fire deep in the dunes of the Sahara, among the same nomads I write about here. It was a magical night, one I will never forget, just as I will never forget the strength of the women I met in the Sahara when I walked.

This book is my own small way of paying tribute to the fierce honour of desert women. Whether Saharawi or Amazigh, I have never felt so fortunate as I did when I walked amongst them, sharing their life for a time.

The Votive Crown picks up the characters and narrative of The Saharan Queen. It is a saga that continues over several full length novels, and a series I have absolutely loved writing. You can sign up on my website and purchase the novels there, or online, in print, ebook, or audio.

If you enjoyed this small snippet, please do leave a review to help others find it. I can't tell you how much reviews mean!

And if you would like to know more about my own Saharan walk, please go to my website at www.paulaconstant.com, or feel free to purchase *Slow Journey South* and *Sahara,* the books about the Saharan walk, online or in any good bookstore.

ABOUT THE AUTHOR

Between 2004-2007, Paula Constant walked over 12000km through eight countries, including 7000km through the Sahara with her own camels and only local nomads for support. She wrote two books about her journey, Sahara and Slow Journey South, both published by Random House. The Visigoths of Spain series was conceived on that journey. She moved to Granada (Illiberis) in Spain where she lived for two years whilst researching the series. She divides her time between tropical Broome, Western Australia, and southern Spain. If you'd like more free samples, and to stay in touch, go to www. paulaconstant.com, and sign up.